RANGE
WAR

Raymond D. Mason

RANGE WAR

Copyright © 2013 by Raymond D. Mason

All rights reserved. No part of this book may be used or reproduced by any means, graphic, electronic, or mechanical; including photocopying, recording, taping or by any information storage retrieval system without the written permission of the publisher/author except in the case of brief quotations embodied in critical articles and reviews.

Raymond D. Mason books may be ordered through authorized booksellers associated with Mason Books or by going to:
www.amazon.com
www.createspace.com
www.barnesandnoble.com
www.target.com
www.borders.com
:

You may order personalized, autographed books by E-mailing your order to:

RMason3092@aol.com or

(541) 679-0396

This is a work of fiction. All characters, names, incidents, organizations, and dialogue in this novel are either the products of the author's imagination or are used fictitiously.

Printed in the United States of America

Range War

See back pages for other books by this author.

Raymond D. Mason

__Preface__

Identical twins, Brent and Brian Sackett, left the family cattle ranch in Abilene, Texas to fight on opposite sides in the War Between the States. After the War Brent still harbored hard feelings towards his brother and did not return to their ranch. Instead, Brent took a job as a deputy sheriff.

Brian did return to the family ranch, but when the eldest Sackett son, AJ, was seriously wounded Brian set out in search of the man he thought was responsible. His pursuit took him all the way to Laredo, Texas where he caught up with the man, but too late. The man had been killed by the sheriff of Laredo.

About that same time, Brent had absconded with money stolen in a freight office holdup, killing the sheriff in the process. Brent was now a man on the run. His flight brought about more shootings, thus he was truly a wanted outlaw with a price on his head.

Being identical twins and traveling through the same area of Texas, Brent's action put Brian in harm's way as well. After several close calls, the two brothers wound up in San Antonio, Texas where they confronted each other.

Brent was recognized and arrested, along with Brian since the sheriff was in a quandary over which one was actually the man wanted by the law. When Brent escaped it pointed the finger of guilt at him, thus letting Brian off the hook.

Brian returned to the family ranch, while Brent, on the run from the law, met Julia; a woman whose husband and several others had been killed by cowboys who worked for a ruthless rancher while making a move to Sundown, Texas.

Brent cared for the woman and promised to see to it that she made it to Sundown and the small farm her deceased husband had purchased.

As they were nearing their destination, Brent and Julia ran into two men who had robbed the bank in the small town and Brent was shot and seriously wounded. Julia rushed him on into town where he was attended to by the local doctor.

During this time word reached the Sackett family that Brent might be in Sundown, Texas. John Sackett sent his oldest son, AJ, and Brian to find Brent and help him get across the border to Mexico in order to escape being chased down by a posse somewhere and shot, or hanged for his crimes.

AJ and Brian found Brent and convinced him to return to their ranch if only to say goodbye to his mother and father before striking out to California in hopes of starting a new life. The past, however, has a way of always reappearing when you least expect it.

Our story opens with Lincoln (Linc) Sackett preparing to go to work on the ranch where he has just been hired as a cowhand. Linc had been involved in a little conflict that had gotten another ranch hand fired due to his bullying tactics; tactics that wouldn't work on Linc.

Raymond D. Mason

1

PIMA COUNTY, ARIZONA
JUNE, 1877

LINCOLN SACKETT tightened the cinch on his buckskin gelding and started to climb into the saddle when Buck Benton, the ranch foreman called to him.

"Hold up there, Linc, I need to talk to you," Buck hollered.

Linc turned around and waited for his boss to approach him. He could see the worry lines between Buck's eyes and knew whatever he wanted to talk to him about was serious; at least to Buck, anyway.

"What is it," Linc asked?

Buck walked up next to his new hire and said seriously, "Montana just informed me that Wild Horse Red told him he had seen Jess Latimer down in Bisbee with two hard cases. They'd been drinking heavily and Latimer was bragging about

Range War

what he was going to do to you. Red said the two he was hanging out with was Whitey Haisley and Brice Dalton. They're both bad news."

"I was wondering when we'd be hearing from Jess again. I guess I'll have to ride tall and alert, huh," Linc grinned.

"He's bad news, Linc; I just want you to be careful," Buck said.

"I will, Buck; and thanks for the warning. I'm going out to check on the herd in the north section. I should be back by supper time," Linc said and climbed aboard his horse.

"Yeah, I'm worried about someone cuttin' out some of our beef and herding them to one of the forts. The supply sergeants don't seem to pay much attention to the brands the cattle are sportin' if they can get a good deal. I've complained about it, but it doesn't seem to do much good," Buck said with a frown.

"Yeah, they need beef and they don't care where it comes from," Linc said and then followed that with, "Adios".

Linc reined his horse around and headed for the north section of the big ranch. As he rode along he considered who the ones might be that had been stealing cattle from other ranches in the area. The name that kept coming to mind was Ike Carter.

The thought of Jess Latimer made Linc shake his head negatively. He'd known the first day on the job that he and Latimer would tangle one day, and they had done just that about two weeks earlier. The fight had led to some gunplay and Linc had grazed Latimer's wrist bad enough to send him to a doctor to have it patched up. Latimer would still have use of his right hand, but it would be hard for him to handle a gun with any real speed and dexterity.

Linc had ridden about four miles when he saw a trail of smoke over a ridge. It looked like a campfire, but could also be a fire built for changing the brand on cattle. He reined his horse in the direction of the smoke and just before he topped the ridge, dismounted and tied the bridle reins to some scrub brush.

Staying low to the ground, Linc moved to the crest of the hill and peered down the other side. It was just as he'd thought; it was a fire for branding irons. Linc could only see three men near the fire, but there were four saddled horses tethered near them. The fourth man soon made his presence known when he emerged from behind some rocks.

There were eight head of cattle in a makeshift pen and the men were busy changing the brand on the ninth steer. Without even seeing the men's faces, Linc knew one of the men was Jess Latimer by the way he moved.

The one thing no rancher would tolerate was cattle or horse rustling. One represented the person's livelihood and the other his survival in a hard land. Every cowhand knew what to do when he ran across rustlers of either horses or cattle. Shoot first and ask questions later.

Linc moved away from the crest of the hill and pulled his Winchester from the saddle scabbard. He checked to make sure there was a shell in the barrel and then moved back to the top of the hill. There were only two men doing the brand changing now. Linc wondered where the other two had gotten off too.

Linc scoured the area for any sign of the two men, but was unable to get a fix on them. He didn't like this, not in the least. Perhaps they had spotted him and had not let on about it. The two men could be trying to flank him and get him in crossfire.

He was just about to head back to his horse and move to another location when he spotted one of the men running from a large brushy area to a small rock formation. It was obvious the man was moving in his direction. Figuring they had spotted him, it meant that the other man was more than likely moving in on him from the other side.

Looking around quickly Linc noticed a slightly low spot where he would not be easily seen from a distance. Anyone discovering his location would have to be right on top of him to see him. He didn't waste any time in lying down in the depression. Now he would be able to see either of the men should they approach his position.

Linc lay motionless with the rifle positioned so it would take little movement to fire should the men discover him. He heard nothing but the sounds of nature as he lay in wait. After what seemed like five minutes he heard whispering coming from both sides of the depression where he lay.

"He's got to be around here somewhere," the man to Linc's right whispered.

"Yeah, his horse is right down there," the man to the left of him whispered back.

Linc silently pulled the hammer back on the Winchester in anticipation of being discovered.

"He has to be here unless he's a ghost. He couldn't have gotten past us without being seen...or could he," the man to the right asked?

Noticing the depression, one of the men walked up to where he could look down into it. It was the last thing he ever did. Linc raised the rifle and shot the man in the head. Before the man hit the ground Linc was on his knees and aiming the rifle at the other man.

The two gunshots were simultaneous making a thunderous roar. The two men attending to the cattle grinned as they looked in the direction of the gun shots.

"Sounds like our snooping cowhand got lead from both Charlie and Brice," Jess Latimer said to Whitey Haisley with a grin.

Whitey looked up the hill with a worried look on his face as he replied, "I hope that's the way it was."

Latimer cast a quick glance up the hillside just as Linc crested the hill. The rustler's eyes widened as he recognized the man he'd sworn to kill...Linc Sackett.

"Sackett," Latimer snapped as he dropped the branding iron he was holding and went for his pistol, even though Linc was out of range of the handgun.

Linc fired at the two cattle rustlers as they bolted towards their horses that were tied nearby. His first shot missed, but the second shot hit Latimer in the shoulder, spinning him around and knocking him to the ground. As Linc jacked another shell in the barrel of the Winchester and took careful aim Haisley stopped and pulled his fallen partner to his feet.

Haisley barked, "Come on, Jess."

Linc squeezed the trigger with Whitey in his sight, but the hammer fell on a cartridge dud. Linc quickly jacked another shell into the firing chamber but by then the two men had managed to make it around a rock formation to where their horses were tied.

By the time Linc caught sight of Latimer and Haisley again they were riding hard and out of range of his rifle. Linc picked up the cartridge that had misfired and checked the back of it. The firing pen had hit the cartridge dead center, but it had not gone off. Linc stuck the cartridge into his pocket and turned to look at the two men he'd shot earlier.

He wasn't able to identify either of the men, but he had seen them both on occasion while in the small unnamed settlement about eight miles from the ranch. Naturally, the place he recognized them from was from the only saloon in the settlement; Muldoon's.

Linc found where the men had tied their horses and brought them back to the site of the shootings. He tied the men's bodies across their saddles and after releasing the cattle from the makeshift pen, headed back towards the ranch.

Raymond D. Mason

2

**SUNDOWN, TEXAS
JUNE, 1877**

AJ AND BRIAN SACKETT took turns digging the hole that Brent Sackett would be buried in. The hard ground made the digging difficult, but the two brothers didn't mind. This was for their brother. Finally they completed the digging and Brian climbed out of the hole.

"That should be deep enough, don't you think, AJ," Brian asked?

"Yeah, that's plenty deep," AJ responded.

"Hey, make it deep enough that no varmints can dig me up," Brent Sackett said with a wry grin.

AJ and Brian laughed at Brent's comment as the two of them picked up the five foot log that would be buried in the hole. They dropped the log into the would-be grave and Brent tossed a worn out hat in on top of it.

"That hat has been through the mill," Brent said looking down into the hole.

"Let's fill it up," AJ said and dumped a shovel full of dirt in on the log and hat and then asked Brian, "Did you spell Brent's name right on his headstone?"

Brian did a double take towards his brother as he replied, "Yeah, unless he's changed the way he spells it. You haven't have you, Brent?"

"Nope, still the same," Brent replied.

Brent wouldn't admit it, but he was pleased to know that his brothers were concerned enough about him to come looking for him. They had greeted him as if nothing had changed since before the War that had driven a wedge between them.

Julia walked to the front door of the small ranch house and called out to the three of them, "Breakfast is ready; come and get it."

"You go ahead; I'll finish filling this hole up," AJ said.

"You won't have to say that twice; will he, Brent," Brian said with a laugh?

"Nope; let's go before he wants us to help him," Brent said jokingly.

As the two identical twin brothers walked towards the house, Brian put his arm around Brent's shoulder. He could feel Brent tense slightly, but then relax. It was so good to have Brent 'back in the fold' so to speak; even if it was for just a short spell.

"Once we get back to the ranch maybe we can talk you into staying," Brian said, getting a quick glance from Brent.

"Brian, I can't stay there; not with the law looking for me. My only chance is to go out to California or down to Mexico; and I don't really cotton to living out my days south of the Border," Brent said.

"What I was thinking was building you and Julia a house on the ranch somewhere off the beaten path. You know; a real nice house where one of the line shacks is now. No one would run across you there," Brian continued.

"And not be able to go into town? I'd be living like a hermit. I'm not cut out to live like that. Out in California Julia and I can start over. I'll take a different name and we will simply blend in with the landscape out west. My minds made up, so that's it," Brent said firmly.

"Okay, I won't bring it up again, but Ma and Pa will, you can be sure," Brian answered.

"I know, but they'll understand…I hope."

They entered the house and sat down at the table as Julia brought a platter of friend eggs and sat them down. She had another platter of bacon in her other hand. The boys filled their plates and began to eat. Before they had taken their third bite AJ entered and sat down across from them.

"You're not finished filling the hole out there all ready, are you," Brian asked?

"Nope, the smell of this food took priority over the hole. I'm starving," AJ said, getting a laugh from Brian and Brent.

Once they had finished breakfast, the three of them went back and completed filling the hole that would act as Brent's grave. They placed the

15

headstone at one end of the six foot long grave with the words, 'Here lies Brent Sackett. AKA Dan Johnson; Rest in Peace'.

Brent looked at the headstone and slowly shook his head as he said, "I just hope no one is curious enough to open up the grave."

"I don't think they would be that curious. Just the thought that you had come to the end of your life will be enough, I think," AJ said.

"Well, as soon as Julia has the dishes cleaned up and packed we can load up the table and chairs and be on our way. The further away from here we can get, the better I'll feel," Brent said.

As the three of them turned to go and help Julia, Brian stopped and looked off into the distance. The other two followed his gaze and saw what had stopped Brian in his tracks. It was smoke; and a lot of it.

"That's in the direction of Sundown," Brent said.

"What do you think it is...a prairie fire," Brian asked?

"Either that or...Indians," Brent replied.

"One's about as bad as the other," AJ offered.

"You can't shoot a fire," Brent replied.

"Maybe we ought to wait here until we find out what it is," Brian said.

AJ shook his head, "No, if it's a fire we'd be sitting ducks if we wait here."

Brent stated, "Yeah, and we wouldn't be much better off if it is Indians and they catch us out on the open plains."

Range War

Brian started walking towards his horse and said, "Well, I'll find out what it is so we know what we should do."

"I'll go with you," AJ said and started to follow him.

"No, you wait here with Brent and Julia. I won't be long. Besides, I think it is Indians. A prairie fire would be a lot wider than that smoke," Brian stated.

He climbed aboard his horse and kicked it into an easy gallop in the direction of the small town of Sundown. Hopefully he would meet someone who could tell him what the smoke was all about and he wouldn't have to make the full trip into town.

He had ridden about two miles when he met two covered wagons. They had the horses in a trot and the wagons were loaded with some of the people's belongings, but certainly not much. When they saw Brian they pulled their teams to a halt.

"Where are you folks headed," Brian called to the man driving the first wagon with his wife and two children aboard?

"Comanche war party attacked Sundown. They're burning the town down. We barely got out of there with our lives. Hopefully we can get to the Lubbock County marshal's office before they catch up to us," the man said.

"Thanks, I've got to get back and warn my kin," Brian said and reined his horse around and headed back towards Brent and Julia's place in a full gallop.

When AJ and Brent saw Brian they met him as he stepped off his horse before it had even come to a full stop.

"Comanche war party has attacked Sundown. I met a couple of wagons and they were from town," Brian said.

"It seems to me they would have had better cover in town than out on the open plains," Brent remarked.

"They said the Comanche's were burning down the entire town. They barely got away," Brian repeated what he'd been told.

"I think we'd be better off making a stand here than trying to out run them with the wagon holding us back," AJ said, and then asked, "What do you boys think?"

"I think you're right. We've got enough fire power to hold out for sometime. Let's store up some water inside while we've got time," Brent said, getting an agreeing nod from Brian.

"Yeah, I agree. They may not even head this way, but we'd better to be prepared in case they do," Brian stated.

Brent looked at his two brothers for a moment and then said very seriously, "It's good to be with you two again. I guess I missed your being around me more than I thought."

The two brothers gave Brent a caring smile which spoke much more than any words could say. They both put a hand on Brent's shoulder and the healing of hard feelings began to rapidly take place.

"Well, let's get ready to meet our unexpected guests, should they arrive," AJ said with a slight grin.

The three of them began preparing for an attack by the Comanche war party. They moved as much of the firewood as they could inside the house to make it more difficult for the war party to burn them out. Of course there was always the wood from the wagon and the small barn, the Comanche's could use.

Once they had stored up enough water to last them for sometime, they went outside to wait for the first sighting of the marauding Indians. While they watched they talked.

"Did I tell you boys about the time Ace Tarkington and Sid Holliman said they were going to beat hell out of Pa the next time he went into Abilene," AJ said with a grin?

"No, when did this happen," Brian asked?

"Oh, it was while you both were away. Anyway, Sid and Ace sent word out to the ranch that the next time Pa came into town they were going to get even with him for his firing them.

"Well, we had just hired a guy by the name of Ivan Miller who was from Philadelphia. Now Ivan was a quiet sort; never bothered anybody and no one bothered him. He was pretty mum when it came to talkin' about himself. He'd always deflect questions with a joke of some kind.

"Well, you know how Pa is; when he got word about Sid and Ace's intention he found an excuse to go into town. Ivan had been present when the message was delivered and asked Pa if he could go into town with him to see the doctor. Pa said yes, but, as it turned out there wasn't anything wrong with Ivan; he just wanted to even the odds a little.

"Well, anyway Pa and Ivan rode into town and when they arrived Pa went to the feed store where Pa had heard Ace had gotten a job. Ace wasn't there and Chet Larkin, the storeowner told Pa he'd fired Ace and could probably find him and Sid at the Silver Horseshoe Saloon.

"Pa headed for the saloon with Ivan tagging along. Pa said he asked Ivan about his wanting to see the doctor, but Ivan told him whatever it was that had been ailing him, wasn't hurtin' anymore.

"The two of them walked into the saloon and sure enough, there was Ace and Sid standing at the bar. Pa called to 'em and told 'em he'd heard they wanted to see him. Well, those boys made a beeline for Pa, but when they got about five feet from him, Ivan stepped in front of Pa and cold cocked both of them with one punch delivered to each of their chin's.

"Pa said he was stunned at how quickly Ivan put both of them away and just stood there staring at him. Ivan turned to Pa and smiled and said, 'I guess that ought to quiet them down for awhile'.

"It turned out Ivan had been a prizefighter back in Philadelphia but had quit when he accidentally killed a man during a match. Obviously he wasn't opposed to bustin' someone's head once in awhile, he just didn't want to do it for a living."

"So what happened to Ivan," Brian asked? "I haven't heard his name mentioned until just now. Did he quit?"

"Yeah, he did. He took a job as deputy sheriff down in Coleman. Later he was elected sheriff. As far as I know he's still down there. You'll have to meet him sometime. Whatever you do, though, don't get in a fight with him. Not unless you have a few teeth you don't need anymore," AJ laughed.

3

BLACK JACK HAGGERTY and Four Fingers Frank Jordan rode down Seminole, Texas' main street; population 98. They were tired and hungry and in a bad mood. Short tempers with either man usually spelled trouble.

"We'll get a room for the night, if they've got any spare one's in this one horse town; and then we'll get an early start in the morning," Haggerty said looking down the street ahead for any sign that indicated rooms for rent.

"I want a drink before I do anything. I'll worry about sleep after I've had a couple of drinks," Jordan said evenly; his eyes on a small sign that read simply, 'Saloon'.

"No trouble, Frank! I don't want to have to make a hasty getaway from this so called town," Haggerty said evenly.

"Don't worry about me, Jack. I can handle any trouble that might come my way...or yours," Jordan said unsmilingly.

"That's what I'm afraid of," Haggerty said with a slight grin, and then added. "You go ahead and get your drink and I'll see if I can find us a room."

When they reached the saloon, Jordan reined his horse over to the hitching rail. Haggerty continued on down the street in the direction of a small sign that read 'Rooms'. As Haggerty rode along he looked from one side of the street to the other out of habit. He was always worried that he'd see someone from his past that might be carrying a grudge against him; be it gang member or lawman.

Haggerty had been the leader of several gangs and had never shied away from leaving them to fight off a posse while he made good his escape. Several of his old gang members had put the word out that they were gunning for him for doing that to them.

Black Jack tied up at the small building that had a 'Rooms' sign out front, and pulled his saddle bags and rifle from his horse. He walked inside and looked around for a clerk.

"Hey, is anyone here," Haggerty called out.

A man came out of a small alcove behind the counter and asked, "Can I help you?"

"Give me a room," Haggerty ordered.

"We have four rooms; take your pick. Three down here and two on the second floor," the clerk said.

"I want one with a bed big enough for two of us to sleep in," Haggerty said with a frown.

"That'll be one dollar," the man said.

"One dollar," Haggerty said as he looked around at the dingy surroundings.

Range War

"One dollar...take it or leave it," the man said evenly.

Haggerty reached into his shirt pocket and pulled a silver dollar out and tossed it on the counter.

"What two upstairs are empty," Haggerty asked?

"We only have two up there and they're both empty."

"I'll take the one that looks out onto the street," Haggerty stated.

"Enjoy your stay," the man said without a trace of sincerity in his tone of voice.

"Yeah, right," Haggerty said uninterestedly, and then added. "What idiot would name a town after a tribe of Indians?"

The clerk looked dumbfounded at Haggerty and shrugged his shoulders, "I never thought about it."

"Well, maybe you ought to," Haggerty snapped with a frown, as he mumbled under his breath, "Seminole!"

The outlaw made his way up the stairs and when he reached the top of the landing looked down at the clerk.

"Well, can you answer that question for me," Haggerty asked?

"About the town's name," the clerk asked haltingly?

'Yeah about the town's name; what idiot named this town Seminole?"

"I really don't know," the clerk said.

Haggerty looked at the man for a moment and then replied, "Well, find out and let me know."

23

With that, Haggerty turned and walked to the door that led to the room he'd rented. The clerk scratched his head and said to himself, "I wonder why he's so worked up about the town's name?"

Haggerty went in and stowed his gear in a corner of the room. After testing the bed's softness he walked over to a table that held a water pitcher and a wash bowl and poured some water into the bowl.

Haggerty washed his face first and then proceeded to wash his neck and ears. He took the dirty water over to the window and looked out before he slung the water from the wash bowl all the way out to the street.

"Hey, watch it," someone yelled up from the street.

"You watch it," Haggerty yelled back.

The man who'd come close to getting doused with the water moved out into the street so he could look up at the window from where the water had been thrown. He was wearing a sheriff's deputy badge.

"What's the meaning of dumping that water down here," the deputy asked?

"Where else am I going to dump it," Haggerty snapped back?

"Take it to the end of the hall and dispose of it out the back door; you don't throw it out onto the street," the deputy stated with a frown.

"The back door; you mean this dump has a back door," Haggerty said questioningly?

"Yeah, it does," the deputy answered.

"Well I'll be..., this place actually has a back door," Haggerty said quietly under his breath and then called down factitiously to the deputy, "Thanks for telling me."

"Yeah...sure," the deputy said, and headed on down the street.

Haggerty had just turned away from the window when he heard two gunshots outside. He turned back towards the window and looked in the direction from which the shots had come. His first thought was that Frank Jordan had shot someone in the saloon. He was wrong.

Two men came running out of the Wells Fargo freight office across the street with guns drawn and carrying a Wells Fargo money bag. They were attempting to mount their horses when the deputy Haggerty had been talking to opened fire on them from the opposite side of the street.

The men managed to get aboard their mounts and returned fire in the deputy's direction. One of the Wells Fargo freight clerks appeared in the office doorway with a shotgun, but was gunned down by one of the men.

Haggerty saw one of the bandits take a slug in the shoulder causing him to drop his pistol. The two men kicked their horses into a dead run in an effort to make their getaway. Haggerty watched closely to see which direction they went once they got out of pistol range. They headed west.

Haggerty smiled as he thought of the men getting away with the robbery that he figured couldn't have got them more than a couple hundred dollars. He quickly grabbed his hat and headed out of the room to find out how much they had actually gotten away with.

When Haggerty reached the front of the hotel he found the deputy lying on the boardwalk. The deputy had been wounded in the fracas but was still conscious. Other people had already gathered around him and had sent for the doctor. The downed freight clerk on the other side of the street also had people hovering around him.

Haggerty watched the crowd and when he spotted one of the men from the freight office near the deputy, moved over next to the man.

"Where's the sheriff," Haggerty asked?

"He's down at the jail probably. Someone went for him," the freight clerk said.

"How's the fella over there," Haggerty asked motioning towards the freight office?

"He's dead," the clerk said.

"How much did they get; do you know, yet," Haggerty asked?

"Yeah, they got over two thousand dollars," the clerk stated. "Somehow they knew when we had just gotten a big pay off from one of the ranchers for some goods he'd had delivered from back east."

"What could have cost that much," Haggerty asked?

"Barbed wire," the clerk said. "Two boxcar loads of the danged stuff; delivered to the train station at the Dawson County train depot," the clerk said disgustedly.

"I thought this was mostly open range country around here," Haggerty said wonderingly?

"It is...or should I say it was."

"I take it that the other ranchers are not too happy with the barbed wire being brought in," Haggerty said.

Range War

"Not in the least. There're some bad feelings being created by the barbed wire move. There's even talk of a range war if old man Dutton starts stringing that wire," the clerk offered.

"Dutton...that wouldn't be Ben Dutton, would it," Haggerty asked, fishing for answers?

"No, George Dutton. He owns the biggest spread in these parts and a lot of water."

Instantly Haggerty began to formulate a scheme for making some money off this range war possibility. He saw a way of playing both ends against the middle and making himself a handsome payday. Maybe he and Jordan wouldn't be going all the way out to Arizona after all.

Frank Jordan looked at Haggerty with a perplexed look on his face. He'd just heard the plan Haggerty had formulated, but couldn't see any reason to get excited about it.

"So there may be a range war here; where does that leave us and how does that put any money in our pockets? Are you planning on hiring out our guns," Jordan questioned?

"Think about it, Frank. These ranchers are going to be needing hired guns. We'll provide them with those gunmen and once this war gets underway we take cattle from every rancher in the area and shift the blame over to this Dutton character. We keep the war going until we have a sizeable herd of cattle and that's when we put money in our pockets," Haggerty grinned.

"I ain't no cowhand and I don't like the idea of playing nursemaid to a bunch of cattle. I say we knock off one of the richer ranchers around here and move on," Jordan argued.

"Do you know what cattle are going for right now? Well let me tell you...over twenty five dollars a head. And the buyers from back east ain't interested in how many different brands there might be in a herd they buy. They just want beef for their customers back home. I see a small fortune being made off this coming range war. And I, for one, plan on fanning the flames of war," Haggerty said with a frown.

"So how many head are you talking about?"

"I'd say about a thousand. By the time the ranchers know what's happened we'll have the herd moved to the nearest railhead and be counting a fistful of money," Haggerty said confidently.

"You're talking big money here, Jack...twenty five thousand dollars or more," Jordan said thoughtfully.

"Yep...maybe as much as thirty thousand," Haggerty grinned.

"We'd have to have help in moving that large a herd to the railhead," Jordan replied.

"We won't take 'em all at once. We'll move 'em a hundred or so head at a time. Once we start the range war we'll have the ranchers too busy killing one another to notice the losses to their herds. And again, even if they do we'll lay it off on this George Dutton guy. I'll handle all the details. Now, we've got to start locating some hired guns," Haggerty stated.

4

DAWSON COUNTY TRAIN DEPOT

GEORGE DUTTON walked up to the boxcar and peered in at the spindles of barbed wire. He wore a dour look on his weathered face. He shook his head as he turned his attention from the boxcar loaded with barbed wire to his twenty one year old daughter who was standing beside him.

"I never thought it would come to this point...barbed wire. I hate the stuff, but I've got to protect my property. With these dry conditions I have to worry about my cattle before I do the rest of the ranchers around here," Dutton stated.

"They're not going to like the fact that they're going to have to drive their cattle around our ranch to get them to market. Plus, you're cutting some off from water. This is bound to cause hard feelings and maybe real trouble, Dad," Hannah Dutton said.

"I've had people holding hard feelings against me more times than I care to count. This is a tough business and it calls for drawing a line in the sand sometimes. You know tough times call for tough measures, Honey," Dutton said, calling his daughter by the nickname he'd given her when she was small.

"I know, but I hate the whole thing. I get enough hard stares when I go into town now to do any shopping that needs doing. Maybe the fact that you're planning on putting some gates in the fence will ease people's minds," Hannah said.

"Those gates are for our riders; not just anyone that happens by. No, I'll not have a lot of people crossing our range until this danged dry spell is over and the grass comes back," Dutton snapped.

Just then a man on horseback rode up behind George and his daughter. It was Court Gary, one of the larger ranchers in the Seminole area. His spread was almost as large as Dutton's.

"Admiring your barbed wire, eh, George," Gary asked as he reined up.

Turning around to face Gary, Dutton snapped back, "Yeah, I wanted to make sure they shipped all that I'd ordered...they did."

"You're really going through with this fool notion, are you," Gary said with a frown.

"I am, Court. I've got to protect what's mine and I thought you'd understand that. I can't have people driving their cattle across my land destroying what little grass I have for my cattle due to this dry weather. My cattle can't go thirsty so other rancher's cattle won't," George said testily.

"Do you know how far out of the way I'll have to drive my cattle to get them to market? Well, I'll tell you. It will add over a hundred miles to our drives. A hundred miles over range that's scarce on water and feed," Court said with a deep frown.

"I'm sorry about that, Court. Once the dry season lets up and the grass comes back, I'll think about opening up some wire; but for now it'll stay," Dutton said with finality in his voice.

Court looked at Hannah and asked, "Can't you talk any sense into your dad's head, Honey?"

"No...his mind is made up, Court. I'm sorry for all of this, but sometimes tough decisions have to be made," Hannah said evenly.

"You sound like George. Oh, well...like they say 'you can't argue with just one Dutton'," Court said.

"Who says that," George snapped?

"Everyone," Court said. "Adios. I hope the next time we meet it isn't with guns drawn, but it looks like it might come down to that. There are some hard feelings among the other ranchers, George. They're talking 'range war'."

"If it comes down to that...so be it. We'll be ready for anything you and the others might throw at us," George replied tersely.

Court looked at the two Dutton's for a moment, shook his head slowly, and then reined his horse around and rode off in the direction of Seminole.

Hannah looked worried, "Do you think Court was serious about their being a range war, Dad?"

George thought for a moment and then said in tight words, "I'd say he's absolutely right. And we've got to be ready."

George and Hannah left the loading platform once the freight wagons arrived that was to deliver the wire to their ranch. They mounted up and headed towards a small café the railroad had started for travelers before heading back to their ranch where George would wait for the barbed wire to be delivered.

They had just given the waiter their order when two men entered and looked around the room. When they spotted George and Hannah they marched over to their table.

"Dutton, we ran into Court Gary on the way into town and he said the barbed wire you ordered had arrived. We just left the loading dock at the train station and the wire is being loaded onto the freight wagons now. You know what this means, don't you," the taller of the two men said?

"Yeah, it means my men are going to be stringing some wire, Sherman. I've not made it a secret as to what my plans are," Dutton stated.

"You realize that you're forcing us to do something that none of us want to do, don't you," Sherman said.

"You do what you have to do, and I'll do what I have to do," Dutton said nonchalantly.

"You think you can just run roughshod over us smaller ranchers and we'll lay there and take it, don't you? Well, you're wrong, George. We'll fight you with everything we've got," Sherman said with flashing eyes.

"Do what you must. I'll tell you what I told Gary; if you come out to rip out the wire...you'd better come a shootin'," Dutton snapped.

Range War

"Oh, we will; you can be sure of that. We're sending for some experts in the field. They should start arriving any day now," Sherman said in an effort to run a bluff.

"Two can play that game, Sherman," Dutton said with a slight nod of his head.

"There's going to be a lot of needless blood shed over this move of yours. And the blood will be spilled on both sides of that wire," Sherman said and turned and walked away with his sidekick following him.

When they were out of earshot, the man with Sherman asked, "What do we do now?"

"We make good on the threat I just made. We hire us some guns."

"Where are you going to go to do that? I sure don't know any guns for hire," the man said.

"Neither do I, but we'll find 'em...somewhere."

"Howdy," Haggerty said as him and Jordan rode up to the corral where several cowboys were watching as the ranch owner trained a cutting horse.

"Howdy...if you're looking for work you'll have to talk to the man on the horse there," the ranch hand said motioning towards the man in the corral.

"He's the one I want to speak with then. What's his name," Haggerty asked?

"Royce Bellows," the wrangler said.

After a few minutes Bellows reined the horse over to the corral railing and nodded his head in approval of how the cutting horse had done its job.

"Yep, this one is ready," Bellows said and then noticed the two new arrivals. "What do you two want?"

"We hear that there's a range war brewing; is that right," Haggerty asked?

Bellows looked the two men over before answering, "Yeah, there might be...if old man Dutton goes ahead with stringing barbed wire. Why do you ask?"

"We've seen range wars before. In fact, we've been in range wars before and our side always came out on top," Haggerty said confidently.

"Is that right? So you want to hire out your guns, eh," Bellows stated rather than asked.

"No...we want to wage the war for you. You have a bunch of wranglers working for you; they're not gunmen. Our boys are. That's the reason our side always wins. Our men know what they are doing. Cowboys are good with cows, horses, and ropes; my men are good with pistols, rifles, and dynamite," Haggerty said seriously.

Bellows thought for a moment and then said, "We might be interested. I'll have to talk to the other ranchers. How much is this going to cost us?"

"It'll cost you two hundred fifty dollars a gun hand; five hundred a man if there's actually a shooting war," Haggerty said and then added. "I can tell you one thing...when the other side sees my men, they're not going to be in any big hurry to press a fight."

"There're six ranches that would be siding against the rancher stringing the wire. I think they might go along with that depending on how many men you're talking," Bellows said thoughtfully.

"You tell me how many guns you want and I'll provide them. Let's just say we'll do it for whatever the market will bear," Haggerty said with a grin.

"Where are you staying, Mister…?"

"Hag…Haggard, Wesley Haggard; this is my sidekick, Dynamite Blaine," Haggerty said almost giving the man his real name. "We're staying at the hotel in town; if you can call either of them what I just did. Of course we'll need a couple of days to get our men in here, should the other ranchers be willing to hire our services. We don't all travel together, you know."

"No, I don't guess you would. I'll talk to the others and get to you tomorrow morning. And, you'd better be as good as you say you are, Mr. Haggard," Bellows said seriously.

"Oh, we're every bit as good as I say we are. In fact, I'd say we're the best there is at what we do," Haggerty said with a grin.

Raymond D. Mason

5

AJ SAT ATOP the small farmhouse so he would be able to watch the horizon better. He was watchin for a dust cloud that would indicate the Comanche were headed that way. Brent and Brian Sackett made sure their guns were fully loaded and the necessary supplies were inside the house should the Indians mount an attack.

"Still nothing, AJ," Brian called up to his brother?

"Not yet. With there being no breeze to speak of, any dust they kick up will be easy to spot. Do you think we have enough water inside the house," AJ asked?

"We'd better because we don't have anything else to fill," Brent replied.

AJ started to say something and stopped short. He squinted slightly in order to focus a little better on something he saw in the direction of Sundown. It was a trail of dust drifting lazily into the still Texas air.

"Someone's coming, and coming fast; but it doesn't look like enough dust to be a war party of any size. It's more like a couple of riders," AJ stated.

"We can handle a couple of Comanche with no trouble," Brian said jokingly.

"Hold it...there's a much bigger cloud several hundred yards farther back," AJ said as he continued to watch the approaching dust clouds.

After a few minutes AJ said excitedly, "There're the first riders; looks like four of them. And here come the others...must be thirty or more of them. Get ready boys; we're about to have company."

AJ started climbing down off the roof as the four riders approached the ranch house. The four men pulled their rifles from their saddle scabbards as they dismounted and hit the ground running.

"Comanche war party; about six hundred yards behind us," the lead rider said as he ran up to where AJ, Brent, and Brian were standing.

The first thing the three brothers noticed was the star on the man's vest that read 'Texas Ranger'. They cast a quick look amongst themselves and then AJ said, "Come on; let's get inside."

The seven of them rushed inside the house, closing and bolting the door behind them. Everyone took a position at a window and prepared to open up on the war party when it got within range.

The taller of the Rangers looked in Julia's direction and then looked away before doing a double take.

Range War

"Well, looks like we meet again, Ma'am," the captain said. "Captain Culpepper, remember? We stopped by here awhile back to water our horses."

"Oh, yes, I remember. I figured you would be long gone by now," Julia said.

"Actually we would have been down around Sweetwater, but we got word about the Comanche war party and figured we could be of more use around here. We had to make a run for it out of Sundown when it was overrun with Indians. We were lucky; some folks weren't," Culpepper stated.

"Here they come, Captain," Ranger McNiece called out.

Everyone took aim and once the war party was in range began to fire. Fortunately there were plenty of repeating rifles inside the house, because the Comanche's began to sustain heavy casualties. The accuracy of the Sackett's and the Rangers coupled with the rapidity of the repeating rifles quickly translated to a hasty retreat by the war party.

After two attacks, the Comanche's suddenly pulled back, not only out of range, but out of sight as well. Now it was a waiting game for those in the house.

"What do you suppose they're up to, Captain," Ranger Knapp asked?

"They're regrouping. They'll be back," Captain Culpepper said.

"They might be playing a waiting game now," Brent said. "They don't know if we have water in here or not. If we don't, we'll have to try and get some from the well. That's what they're waiting to find out."

"Are you speaking from experience, or is that merely a guess," Captain Culpepper asked?

"I've been in a few skirmishes with them. I had a good friend who had married a Comanche squaw, but had to kill her when she came at him with a knife during a family squabble," Brent said with a slight grin.

Brent's remark got a few chuckles from the others. The laughter was short lived, however, when they heard gunshots coming from a distance. They all looked at one another with questioning looks on their faces.

The gunshots seemed to be getting farther away from them, thus eliminating the idea that the Indians were attacking again.

"Now what's that all about," Culpepper asked no one in particular?

"Maybe a US Cavalry patrol," Brian said hopefully.

Before long they had their answer and Brian was right. A small company of soldiers rounded a large cluster of underbrush. The lieutenant in charge held up his hand for the troopers to stop as he rode up to the farmhouse.

AJ went out the door first with the others close behind him. He smiled at the lieutenant with a greeting, "Man, are we glad to see you."

"How long did you have to fight the war party off," the lieutenant asked?

"Not long at all. They made two passes and then retreated," AJ answered.

The lieutenant looked past AJ at the first man behind him and spoke, "Captain Culpepper...is that you?"

"It sure is Lieutenant. You're a welcome sight, I must say. I thought you had led your column south of here," Culpepper commented.

"I did, but we ran across a man who said he'd just left Yellow House Canyon and had heard about a Comanche war party being spotted north of Sundown. We reversed our course and it's a good thing we did," the lieutenant replied.

"How'd you manage to handle the war party so quickly," Brian Sackett asked?

"They scattered to the four winds, making it unwise to break up and give chase. They'll undoubtedly reform somewhere, but from the looks of things here, the war party won't be nearly as large," the lieutenant said as he looked around at the dead bodies.

"Fortunately we picked a good house to hold up in," Captain Culpepper said looking at the three Sackett men.

The lieutenant nodded and gave each of the Sackett's an appraising look. When his gaze fell on Brent and then Brian he smiled.

"Am I seeing double or are you two identical twins," the lieutenant asked?

"There's nothing wrong with your eyesight, Lieutenant," Brian replied.

Brent suddenly realized that he was putting himself in 'harms way' by being seen here with his brother. It would only be a matter of time until someone put two and two together and came up with a man on the run that just happened to have an identical twin brother.

Quickly Brent cast a worried look towards Brian. The lieutenant provided the reason for Brent's worried look.

"What are your names; just out of curiosity," the lieutenant asked?

"I'm Dan Johnson and this is my brother Dean," Brent said before anyone else could answer.

"Dan and Dean...that sounds like names a family would pin on twins," the lieutenant replied.

Captain Culpepper frowned slightly as the names soaked in. He looked at Brian and then at Brent with a look of concern etched on his face. The captain looked at each of his rangers to see if the names registered with any of them, but no one showed any interest.

"That name rings a bell. I could swear I've heard it somewhere before," Culpepper said thoughtfully.

"You've probably heard my name, Captain," Brian said quickly. "I was involved in a shooting down near San Antonio not too long ago. A young man tried to kill me and shot and killed his sister. I'm sure it was carried over the telegraph wires," Brian went on.

"I do remember hearing about that. It was Royce Rawlings son, Buster who shot and killed his sister Barbara. I knew the family and was shocked at the news, but not surprised that Buster finally got around to killing someone. I'm just so saddened that it was Barbie. She was a sweet young thing. That must have been where I heard your name," the captain said.

Brian looked at Brent and could see the relief register on his brother's face. Now if the good captain didn't start pressing his memory for what the man's name really was that Buster tried to shotgun to death. The name everyone down there had heard was his real name, Brian Sackett.

"And how are you related to these two," the captain asked AJ.

"I'm their cousin, AJ Sanders," AJ said, not wanting to get in on something that he might mess up.

"Sanders...Sanders," Captain Culpepper said thoughtfully, "Say, you're not related to Juke Sanders are you?"

AJ looked quickly at his two brothers and said, "Nope, afraid not."

Culpepper had made up the name of Juke Sanders in an effort to see if he could get AJ to slip up. It hadn't worked so he dropped it.

"Well folks, I'd like to stand here and talk longer, but we'd better get a move on," the lieutenant said as he climbed aboard his mount.

"Good luck, Lieutenant," AJ said, getting an agreeing from the others.

"Take care folks; you too, Captain Culpepper," the lieutenant said and then gave the command for his men to follow him.

"We'd better be moving along also," Captain Culpepper said and then called to one of his rangers. "Sandy, you and Gene see if you can round up our horses."

"Let us help, Captain," Brian said quickly. "Our horses are in the barn."

Raymond D. Mason

6

ONCE THE RANGERS' horses were rounded up they said goodbye and struck out towards Sundown to see what was left of the town. The Sackett boys wasted no time getting on their way to Abilene. They didn't want to take any chances on Captain Culpepper returning should he remember that he'd heard the name Brian Sackett in connection with Barbie Rawlings being shot by her brother Buster.

Brent was very reflective as he drove the covered wagon with Julia seated next to him. He would look at her from time to time and couldn't help but smile. She was a woman like none he'd ever known. He'd heard it said that a man needs a good woman if he's ever going to amount to anything, and he truly believed it now.

What he'd heard Brian say about this Buster Rawlings killing his sister in an attempt to gun down Brian bothered him. That same thing could have happened to Julia when Four Fingers Jordan recognized him and the shootout had occurred.

Brian rode up along the wagon and grinned at Brent, "I thought my heart would stop when that Lieutenant started asking about our names, didn't yours?"

"Yeah, I was scared to death he would keep talking about us being twins and jog the captain's memory about me having a twin brother," Brent said.

Just then AJ rode back towards them and held up his hand for them to stop. Brent reined the team of horses to a halt and Brian pulled up his mount.

"What is it," Brent called out?

"I'm not sure. There's about ten or twelve wagons up ahead and it looks like they've camped for the night. I know we haven't traveled far, but would you feel better if we made camp with them? It would sure be safer just in case that war party regroups. What do you think," AJ asked?

"Normally I'd say let's push on, but I don't want to take a chance with Julia along," Brent said quickly.

"I'm with Brent," Brian said.

"Okay, then we'll hook up with them. At least for the night...I doubt that they're going to Abilene. Traveling with them sure will be safer, that's for sure," AJ said.

Meanwhile, Black Jack Haggerty filled out one telegram form after another as he stood at the desk in the Seminole telegraph office.

When he finished he handed the small stack to the telegrapher and said, "Send these off right

Range War

away. I have a room at the hotel down the street so let me know as soon as any replies come in."

"I'll have our delivery boy bring them to you. What room are you in," the telegrapher asked?

"Just leave them at the front desk, but make sure they're in envelopes; I don't want that nosey clerk reading them," Haggerty said with a frown.

"He would too; I ought to know, he's my brother-in-law. I thought my wife was a gossip; he makes her look like she's had her tongue cut out," the man said.

"Yeah," Haggerty said and then asked, "How much do I owe you?"

"That'll be one dollar for all the telegrams. You can tip the delivery boy."

Haggerty tossed a silver dollar on the counter and walked out. He stopped on the narrow boardwalk and looked up and down the street. He had just turned and started for the saloon that was about four doors down when a lone rider caught his eye.

Giving the rider a long look a grin slowly came to Haggerty's face.

"Sam Sterling...now there's a man who will hire out his gun. Lady Luck is smiling on this venture all ready," Haggerty said to himself.

Haggerty watched as the hired gun reined his horse into the hitching rail in front of the saloon. It had been awhile since Haggerty had seen Sterling and hoped there weren't any bad feelings lingering from their last meeting. It had ended with the two of them having harsh words as they parted company.

Sterling adjusted his gun belt as he entered the saloon. Haggerty hurried down the boardwalk in an effort to get inside the saloon before Sterling could order a drink. It would make their meeting a little easier if he bought Sterling his first drink.

Sterling had walked up to the bar and had to wait while the bartender tapped a keg of beer. Haggerty knew better than to walk directly up behind Sterling due to the fact that his old gang member was a little on the jumpy side.

"Well, I'll be hanged if it isn't my old friend Sam Sterling," Haggerty said when he was a good eight feet from where Sterling was standing.

Sterling looked around with a scowl on his face which he held even after recognizing Haggerty. The two men stared at one another; Haggerty smiling and Sterling wearing a frown.

"Hello, Jack," Sterling finally said tightly.

"Sam, you're not going to believe this, but I was just thinking about you. How would you like to make some money...a lot of money," Haggerty asked?

"Another one of your schemes, Jack; as I recall we had harsh words over your last scheme...remember?"

"Hey, that was my mistake. I'll make it up to you this time," Haggerty said as he walked up to the bar next to Sterling. "Let's take that table over there so we can talk in private."

Sterling eyed Haggerty suspiciously, but followed him over to a table in a corner of the barroom. They sat down and Haggerty called out loudly, "Hey, barkeep...when you get that keg tapped bring us a couple of beers over here."

Range War

Sterling still wasn't overly thrilled about seeing his one time gang leader. He felt he had been shorted several hundred dollars after one of the jobs the gang had pulled and his motto was 'fool me once, shame on you; fool me twice...and I'll kill you.'

"So what is this big deal you got brewing, Jack," Sterling asked?

"How would you like to hire out your gun for several hundred dollars and then share in maybe as much as twenty to thirty thousand dollars," Haggerty asked in a low voice?

"Keep talking...you might convince me," Sterling said showing some interest.

Haggerty explained his scheme to Sterling who could see the possibilities of making a good amount of money from it. Sterling also knew of two more men whose guns were for hire that were in the area; one as near as forty miles away.

"You get a hold of your boys and I'll pick up a few more. I have a good feeling about this coming range war. I've contacted the boys we'll need and as soon as they get here I'll kick this war off with a bang. Tell your boys to get here as soon as possible. We're going to have to work fast on this," Haggerty said with a sardonic grin.

****

"We barely got out of Sundown alive," the wagon master stated. "It's only because we had received word that there was a large war party headed our way."

"How many were in the war party that attacked Sundown," Brent asked curiously?

"We were told there were around a hundred braves in the war party. I'm not sure how many were actually in it, because we all cleared out just before they got there," the wagon master stated.

"It sure wasn't that many that hit our place. There were no more than two dozen that hit us," Brent said with a frown.

"Do you think the Comanche's split up," the man asked?

"That would appear to be the case. If that's what they did, the cavalry patrol that showed up may have headed straight into a trap," Brent said, looking at his brothers.

"Yeah...they wouldn't know what hit 'em," Brian replied. "Let's pray that's not what happened."

"Well, you folks are more than welcome to travel along with us until you have to turn towards Abilene," the man said. "By the way, my name is Corker, Jed Corker."

"My name is AJ Sackett and this is..." AJ started to say his brother's names, but caught himself in time to give the false handles they'd adopted. "Dan and Dean Johnson," he offered.

"So where are you folks headed," the wagon master asked AJ?

"We're on our way to Abilene. We'd feel a lot better traveling a ways with you folks. We'll stay with you as far as Dawson County," AJ said.

"I wish it could be longer, but if that's where we part company, so be it. We can always use more firepower should we need it," Corker said. "Just pull in behind the last wagon over there and I'll introduce you to the others."

"Thanks a lot," AJ said.

Once Corker had moved away from them, Brian looked at AJ with a grin on his face and said, "That was quick thinking about our names. I was about to ask you who you were talking about."

Brent grinned slightly and added, "I came up with the names and I was taken aback for a moment."

Julia looked from one brother to the next and slowly shook her head. Brent noticed and asked, "What is it?"

"You three...boy are you cut from the same cloth," she said with a chuckle.

The brothers looked at one another and nodded their head's in agreement.

"Yeah, I guess we are," AJ said. "Man...what a waste of good cloth."

Everyone broke into laughter. Brent was starting to reestablish himself with the family and it felt good. Old wounds were being healed and hurts forgotten. Hopefully this was the beginning of 'new' beginnings for the man on the dodge. And Brent owed it all to one person; Julia and her unconditional love for him.

Raymond D. Mason

7

GEORGE DUTTON stood looking at the four wagons loaded down with barbed wire. He checked to make sure all the men assigned to taking the wire to the various areas that he wanted to fence off were present. Once he'd counted heads he stood up on the back of one of the wagons and shouted out his orders.

"I want you each one to go out and drop the wire at your assigned spots. One spindle space equally apart just like I explained at the meeting last night. If you run into any trouble, you get back here and let me know immediately. I'll get some of the men out there right away to see to it that the wire gets strung.

"I've heard the rumor that there have been some hired guns brought in by the other ranchers; some say they are 'Regulators'. Well, I've got some men on the way, also. I talked to a man a few days ago who says he'll provide us with all the firepower we'll need to get this job done.

"His name is Sam Sterling. He should be getting out here sometime today with some of his men," Dutton explained.

"I sure hope this doesn't turn into a range war," Jeff Kennedy, one of the ranch hands said just loud enough for Dutton to hear him.

"What was that, Jeff," Dutton called out?

"I hope this doesn't turn into a full out range war. I've been in one and I don't want to be in another one. I saw one time friends trying to kill one another. It got so you didn't know who you could trust," Kennedy yelled out.

"If you have any qualms about fightin', then maybe you'd better mount up and ride out now," Dutton said.

"I didn't say I wouldn't fight, George. I just hope it doesn't come down to that," Kennedy repeated himself.

"I'm not fightin'. I didn't sign on here to kill or be killed in a range war. This barbed wire was a bad idea from the start. If you'll give me what I've got coming to me, I'll be riding out," a ranch hand named Strickland said.

"Same here; I ain't gettin' myself killed over barbed wire," another ranch hand said.

"See my daughter and she'll give you what you have coming. She's up at the house," Dutton said with a deep frown.

As the two men headed off in the direction of the Dutton ranch house, George said loudly, "If there're anymore who want to leave, now is the time to do so. Once this war starts, if it does, I'll shoot anyone who tries to leave. I'll need every one of you to win this ruckus."

Range War

The other men looked at one another, but no one else walked away. Dutton looked around the gathering and then stated, "I'll see to it that you all get a bonus once this is over and we take a herd to market."

Just then five riders rounded the corner of the ranch house and rode up to where Dutton and the others were gathered. It was Sam Sterling and the hired guns he'd been able to contact.

They rode up to where Dutton was and stopped, "These are some of the 'soldiers' we'll be using for this war that's about to start. I want one of them to be in charge of five of your men, Dutton," Sterling said forcefully.

"What do you mean, 'be in charge'," Dutton questioned?

"Just what it sounds like; I want your men to follow my men's orders up to and after the time the shooting starts. I'm not going to have men shot up because your men didn't know what to do," Sterling snapped.

"Oh, yeah...I can see that," Dutton said to Sterling and then called out to his men. "Men, listen up. Which ever one of these men you are assigned to work with, you listen to what they tell you to do. No questions asked, do you hear me," Dutton called out.

The men all nodded that they understood, although a few of them grumbled slightly under their breath. Sterling watched the grumblers suspiciously. He had to be one hundred percent sure of the men who would be taking orders from him and his men if this scheme of Haggerty's was to come off.

55

"Do you men have a problem," Sterling asked as he glared at the grumblers.

"No...we were just wondering what your qualifications are that you would be giving us orders during a range war, that's all," one of the men spoke up.

"Because this is our business, that's why. We've been through these things before and we know how to handle them. If you think you can do a better job, let's hear your qualifications," Sterling snapped and then added. "How many range wars have you been in, hoss?"

"None," the man said dropping his eyes and glancing at those around him.

"Then you'd do well to listen to what we tell you. Mr. Dutton, are you satisfied with our position on this matter," Sterling asked?

"I am. I wouldn't have agreed to it in the first place if I hadn't been," Dutton said.

"Then it's settled," Sterling said as a slight grin pulled at his mouth.

Meanwhile, Black Jack Haggerty was conducting his own meeting amongst the ranchers opposed to Dutton stringing the barbed wire. He and Frank Jordan were laying down their orders as well.

"If you want to come out on top of this brewing range war, gentlemen, you'll have to follow our orders to the letter. We've been in these before and know what works and doesn't work. Is that clear," Haggerty said.

"It is...as long as your orders don't conflict with the running of our ranches. We stand to lose a lot

Range War

of our herds if this wire gets strung. We can't and won't do anything that will cost us more cattle. A number of us could be wiped out," Court Gary said.

"Have you heard the old saying, 'there's safety in numbers'," Haggerty asked?

"Yeah, I have; isn't that what we're doing with this meeting; gathering a number of us to stand against the stringing of the wire," Gary said with a slight frown?

"That applies to your herds as well. What you have to do is run your herds together; not all of the cattle, just enough to make one huge herd. By making one massive herd Dutton can't possibly stop it.

"We'll pick one point to hit along the line of wire. We'll put our men to work ahead of the herd and they'll clear the way at that particular spot. By the time Dutton can gather his men to come against us, we'll be well on our way to the watering holes. Once we've busted through the wire there's no stopping us. And once those cattle get the scent of water there'll be no stopping them," Haggerty stated.

"Moving the herds together won't be an easy task. We're scattered out all over the area here. How do you propose on doing that," Gary asked as the other ranchers nodded their head's in agreement to his question.

"My men and I will handle that. We'll move small amounts at a time so Dutton doesn't get suspicious of what we're planning. As soon as I pick the spot along the line of wire that is the most vulnerable, we'll move the cattle to a point close to it, but keep them out of sight.

"I'm going out and scout out that point as soon as this meeting is over. It's going to be up to you all to make sure you don't give the location of the cattle away. I'm sure Dutton would love to know what we're planning, so it has to be kept a secret until such time as we move," Haggerty stated.

Court Gary was pondering the plan and could see that it sounded like a good plan. He still had his doubts, however. Running the herds together would be a lot of work when it came time to sorting them all out. All the brands mingled in one massive herd? It might work; it had to work.

"Okay, Haggard," Gary said, calling Haggerty by the name they knew him as. "We'll do as you say. Let us know when and where you are moving the cattle to and we'll go along with it."

"Like I said; Dutton can't learn about this, so my men and I will be the only one's who actually know the whereabouts of the cattle; is that understood?"

Gary looked at the other ranchers who held doubtful expressions on their faces. He could tell they didn't like the idea of turning over a number of their cattle to a man they hardly knew. Still, they were in no position to argue since their entire herds were at risk due to the lack of water and feed.

"Look...you aren't risking your entire herds on this; merely a portion. It'll work; you'll see. Dutton will be the only loser on this proposition. He's got water and he's got feed. It's not like we're going to take his ranch away from him," Haggerty said sternly.

"I know, I know...and like you said, what do we have to lose. Okay, just keep us posted on what you want us to do. So how many head of cattle do you want from each rancher? The others are going to want to know," Gary asked?

"How many would you say you all have total," Haggerty asked?

Gary thought for a few seconds and made an educated guess, "I'd say around twenty thousand head; all totaled."

"We can do this with...let's say thirty percent of each rancher's herd. That would make one herd of six thousand head. There's no way Dutton can stop six thousand head of cattle, I don't care how many men he has along that wire line," Haggerty grinned.

What Haggerty was planning was cutting about nine hundred head out of that six thousand for him and his men; of course he would take the lion's share of the money, but every one of his men would get a good payday.

Raymond D. Mason

8

FRANK JORDAN sat across the table from Jack Haggerty with a big smile on his face. Haggerty had just finished going over what they would do once they had moved all the cattle the ranchers were turning over to them into a small valley near Dutton's range land.

"I found the perfect spot for us to hold the cattle in that we're going to be getting from the ranchers. It's in a gorge with only one way in. We'll post two men at the entrance to keep any nosy people out of there until we're ready to move them to market," Haggerty stated.

"How many head will it be," Jordan wanted to know?

"I'm figuring fifteen percent; that would make our herd around nine hundred. I hear the cattle buyers are giving between twenty five and thirty dollars a head. So even if we got as low as twenty dollars we'll still be getting around eighteen thousand dollars. Not bad for about two weeks work, eh," Haggerty said.

"I'll say. Hey, this cowboying ain't all that bad," Jordan laughed. "I didn't realize they could make so much money...but then I guess not too many of them knew it either."

"Once we've got our cattle cut out and in the box canyon, we'll move the main herd to a narrow pass where the wire has been strung. It won't take much to start a stampede and the cattle will remove a major portion of that wire when they bust through it. We'll let Sterling's men and our guys have at it.

"Meanwhile we'll be moving our cattle to market. Old man Dutton will come after the other ranchers and Sterling's boys and the ones we have spooking the herd will keep each other pretty busy. The longer they're shootin' it out, the longer we have to get our cattle to market. By the time they figure out what happened we'll be counting our money and on our way to Arizona. This is turning into one sweet deal," Haggerty grinned.

"I've gotta hand it to you Jack, this is one of your better ideas. I wasn't sure of it to start with, but the more I've seen it take shape the more I like it," Jordan said honestly.

"I'll have to agree with you there. It is one of my better schemes," Haggerty nodded.

PIMA COUNTY, ARIZONA

"Linc, I want you to go into town with me," Buck Benton called to Lincoln Sackett.

"What town would that be," Linc asked?

"It doesn't even have a name... why," Buck replied?

"I wouldn't call that place a town. There're only about seventy five to eighty people living there," Linc chuckled.

"Last count was closer to ninety," Buck grinned.

"A metropolis," Linc laughed. "What do you want me to go with you for; don't tell me you're wanting me to go along so I can bring you home after you tie one on," Linc questioned, only half kidding?

"No, the territorial marshal sent word that he'll be there and wants to talk to you about the two men you killed who were changing the brands on our cattle."

"I told that guy they call 'constable' everything; why doesn't the marshal just ask him," Linc questioned?

"He wants to hear it from you, I guess. Anyway, I have to pick up some things at the Feed Store and you can help me get it back to the ranch. Besides, I want to talk to you and the ride in will give me the chance," Buck went on.

"Okay, whatever you say, Buck. Just let me grab something from my saddlebags. I'll just be a minute," Linc said and walked to where his saddle was resting atop the corral fence.

Linc took something from his saddlebags and walked back to the buckboard where Buck was waiting. When he climbed aboard, Buck questioned him.

"What was that you got out of your saddlebags?"

"Nothing...nothing at all," Linc said innocently.

"It looked like a bottle of some kind; kind of like a bottle of perfume," Buck grinned widely.

"An empty bottle of perfume...I mean cologne. I want to pick up a bottle of the same stuff, but I can't even pronounce the name, so I'll just match the labels."

"You've got a gal; you son of a gun...you've got yourself a gal," Buck said and let out a laugh.

"Keep it under your hat, Buck. I don't want the whole world to know it. Let me break the news when I think the time is right," Linc said with a friendly frown.

"You can tell me, Linc. I won't tell any of the boys who you're sweet on. Let me guess; it's that Corbett gal, right," Buck asked laughingly?

"Nope, it ain't her. Come on let's just get going to Muldoon's," Linc coaxed.

"Oh, I know who it is; it's the Sullivan girl; yep that's who it is. Hey, she's a pretty young thing; a little buck toothed, but pretty in spite of it," Buck went on seriously.

"No that ain't who it is either, Buck. Let's go," Linc said.

"Okay, okay but promise you'll tell me before we get back here to the ranch," Buck said.

"I'll think about it. I ain't saying anymore than that, Buck," Linc said with finality in his voice.

The two headed into the small settlement that would soon become known as Tombstone, although they had no way of knowing that at that time. There wasn't much there, but that would change shortly with the discovery of silver and the opening of a number of silver mines.

Range War

When Linc and Buck arrived in the small settlement they stopped at the only feed store first, to get what was needed there. From there they went to Muldoon's, the only bar in town, figuring to have a drink before meeting up with the territorial marshal.

The moment they entered the barroom you could feel the tension in the room begin to build. Sitting in a corner was none other than Jess Latimer and Whitey Haisley. Jess and Linc's eyes locked onto one another's and a hard stare down got started. Buck and Haisley were soon giving one another hard looks as well.

Before any real trouble got started, however, the territorial marshal and his deputy entered. When he saw Buck; whom he had met before; the two of them headed in Linc and Buck's direction. Their entrance broke Latimer's concentration on Linc, and alerted Linc to the arrival of the lawmen.

"Hello Buck," Jed Hester, the marshal said; Hester was a tall thin man with a handlebar moustache.

"Howdy Jed; what is it you wanted to talk to Linc, here, about," Buck said nodding in Linc's direction?

Linc looked at the marshal and then gave Latimer another quick look before saying, "I hope you were going to ask me about those two sitting over in the corner, Marshal. They are the ones who were helping the two men I shot steal our cattle. Latimer is still wearing a sling over the shoulder I shot him in when he tried to escape," Linc stated.

The marshal followed Linc's gaze and then shook his head no and replied, "I heard the story a little bit different than the way you explained it to the local constable."

Linc's eyes flashed hot with anger, "Just what did you hear from him."

"The way he got the story from Jess and Whitey over there, you jumped the four of them while they were in the process of rounding up some of Ike Carter's cattle. They both barely got away with their lives after you gunned down the other two wranglers," Marshal Hester said.

"I don't care what those two liars said, Marshal. It went down just the way I told this stink hole of a town's constable. Those two over there got away all right, and left behind the penned up cattle that they had already changed the brand on. I drove the cattle with the altered brands back to the ranch and Buck can vouch for it," Linc snapped.

"He's right, Jed. The brands had been changed to appear to be Ike Carter's brand, but you can see a difference. I figure Ike was fixing to drive some cattle to market and wanted a few of ours to add to his herd. If you've got a bone to pick with anybody, start with those two jayhawkers over there," Buck said motioning in Latimer and Haisley's direction.

Latimer had slowly gotten to his feet as he honed in on the conversation between the marshal and Sackett. Whitey Haisley, however, had remained seated with one hand on the table and the other hidden by the table top.

"What was that about us," Latimer called out getting the marshal's attention.

"You just stay where you are, Jess; I'll handle this," the marshal answered back.

Range War

"It doesn't look like you're doing too good a job of handling it from where I sit, Jed," Latimer snapped back.

Buck cut into the conversation at this point, "If you want to see the altered brands, come on out to the ranch. We kept the cattle penned up just in case there was a dispute like this."

"It looks like I'll have to do just that. Jess, if the brands have been altered, I'll be a wanting to talk to you and Haisley there," the marshal said nodding towards the still seated Whitey.

Whitey looked up at his partner and then back in the direction of the lawmen and Linc and Buck. A contorted grin creased his face just before he suddenly pulled his hidden hand out from under the table; a hand filled with his .44 Army Colt.

The gun roared as a flame leaped from the barrel. Whitey got off two shots before the others could get their guns drawn. The first bullet hit the marshal in the shoulder, spinning him around and knocking him to the barroom floor. The second one hit the deputy in the rib cage, sending him flying against the wall and then to the floor.

Linc and Buck had both filled their hands and had returned fire at this point. Linc's bullet hit the standing Latimer in the chest, killing him almost instantly. Haisley had gotten to his feet and was moving towards the lone window in the back of the small barroom.

Buck fired at Whitey, but missed. It gave Whitey just enough time to dive through the opened window. Linc had gotten one more shot off after having killed Latimer; the bullet had caught the heel of Haisley's boot, knocking it off.

67

Whitey and Latimer had tied their horses up in back of the saloon so Whitey was in the saddle and riding away fast by the time Linc and Buck reached the window.

"Whitey is headed for the Carter ranch you can be sure of it," Buck said.

"Do you want to go after him," Linc asked quickly?

"No, let him go. We'll let the law handle him and the Carter's. We won't have any trouble getting them to believe your side of the story as to what happened out there now. We can thank Whitey Haisley for that," Buck grinned as he nodded in the direction Whitey had headed.

The wounds of the marshal and the deputy were serious, but not life threatening. The deputy had actually received the more severe wound of the two. The incident had proven Linc's story was the one to be believed. It also put a target on Linc's back and a price on his head. Ike Carter would see to that.

9

BRIAN AND AJ SACKETT rode along together and talked about what they thought might happen when they all got back to the ranch. They both knew that their pa would do everything he could to keep his son out of prison.

The one thing that worried the two of them, however, was Brent insisting on going out to California. They knew it would just be a matter of time until the law caught up to him out west.

Brent looked at the woman seated on the wagon seat by his side and couldn't help but smile. She was definitely a 'godsend' in his eyes. Julia was everything he'd ever thought a woman should be. The longer he knew her, the more his thoughts were confirmed.

Julia looked at Brent and cocked her head to one side, "Now what are you thinking, Brent..." she paused and teasingly looked around as if someone might over hear,"...Sackett," she whispered?

"I was just thinking how pretty you are. I had a little sorrel mare one time that I thought was the most beautiful animal on four legs. You remind me of that little mare," Brent said.

Julia raised her eyebrows as she grinned and said, "Oh, thanks a lot...so you think I'm as pretty as a horse, is that it?"

Brent looked shocked for just a moment before saying, "No, no...I didn't mean it that way. You're prettier than a horse," he sputtered.

"Oh, oh...so you were serious. I'm prettier than a horse," Julia went on, knowing full well how Brent had meant the compliment.

"No, I mean yes, of course you're prettier than a horse; any horse...oh, you know what I meant to say, honey," Brent said flustered.

Julia laughed unable to contain it, "I know what you're trying to say, and thank you, Brent. I was just having some fun with you."

Brent grinned, "Let me put it this way. If there are beautiful angels in heaven, they all must look like you."

"Now that is a compliment I can live with. As long as the angels don't look like horses," Julia said with a chuckle.

Just then Brian rode up alongside the wagon. He grinned when he saw how Julia had changed Brent's demeanor from the time he'd met up with his twin in San Antonio. For that reason alone, Brian felt endeared to Julia. Brent was more like the twin he'd grown up with before the War.

"We should be getting close to the cutoff to Abilene. There maybe a general store there. One of

Range War

the men in a wagon up front said there was the last time he came through here," Brian asked?

"I could use more flour and we're getting low on coffee and sugar," Julia smiled.

"Yeah, and I need a beer," Brent said with a grin. "Did he say if they sold beer or not?"

"He didn't say, but I'm sure we could all use one of them," Brian laughed in reply.

"Don't forget me," Julia said joining in.

"How could we ever forget you, honey," Brent said, certainly not joking.

"I'll go ahead and talk to the wagon master and let him know that we'll be taking the left fork when we get to the cutoff. He say's he knows a big rancher down this way by the name of Dutton," Brian said just as AJ rode up alongside him.

"What about Dutton? Did he say the man's name was George Dutton," AJ asked seriously?

"I think that's what he said the man's first name was," Brian replied. "Why, have you heard of him?"

"Yeah, he came to the ranch almost a year ago. George Dutton; I'm sure that's the man's name. Dutton and his daughter came to look at a couple of horses we had for sale. She was a cute little filly as I recall," AJ stated.

"What the horse, or the gal," Brian said getting a laugh from Brent.

"What is it with you Sackett men always comparing women to horses," Julia said with a mischievous grin, watching Brent out of the corner of her eye?

71

"Now you've done it," Brent said and chucked again. "I just got out of a jam because of it and you put us right back in to it."

"It's because we think so highly of good horse flesh," AJ said trying to soothe the unintended slur.

"Oh, well that explains everything," Julia said as she rolled her eyes.

"This is where I came in," Brent said and climbed off the wagon seat and onto the back of Brian's horse with him.

"I'll go with you to talk to the wagon master. AJ, you can stay here and dig the holed deeper that you've dug for yourself," Brent laughed.

George Dutton supervised the stringing of the wire along the trail that led to the Abilene cutoff. He had ridden along the entire route when the post holes had been dug and now was making sure the wire got strung properly. He didn't want any herds that were being driven to market crossing his land and the wire would see to it that it didn't happen.

"That looks good, Jim," Dutton said to one of his regular hands.

Jim nodded and looked at Sterling's man making sure that no one interfered with the wire being strung.

"Boss, I don't trust these men you've got guarding us. I swear these men are on the dodge from the law," Jim said.

Dutton looked at the men that Sterling had guarding his ranch hands, "Why do you say that? I know they look tough, most hired guns do; but, that doesn't mean they're on the run from the law."

"That one down the line there is. I know I saw a wanted poster on him hanging on the wall in the sheriff's office in Santa Angela the last time I was there," Jim said.

Dutton looked at the man pointed out to him. The man certainly had a hard look about him. What could his men expect, though? This was a job that not just anyone would even take on. Most of his ranch hands wouldn't want to engage in a range war. They were cowboys, not gunmen.

"I'll keep an eye on them, Jim. You just keep stringing that wire, okay," Dutton said.

"I will, boss; I just wanted you to be aware of how me and some of the other men feel," Jim said.

Dutton nodded his head knowingly as he kicked his horse up and headed down the wire line to the next group of men.

Royce Bellows watched as Haggerty and Jordan along with another man they'd hired began moving the cattle he was donating to the large herd that would be used to crash the wire line.

As the cattle donated by Bellows were being herded away from the rest of his herd, Bellows shook his head negatively. He wasn't happy about turning over 30 percent of his herd to a man he'd just met. Even if Haggard, as Bellows knew him by, was running the show for the impending range war, he still didn't like the deal.

Haggerty rode over to where Bellows was sitting astride his horse observing the cutting out process. Haggerty could see that Bellows was not happy about this and quickly moved to settle his fears.

"I'll keep you posted on a daily basis as to the progress on this whole thing, Mr. Bellows. Once we get the cattle gathered from the other ranchers we'll move and move quickly. I want to catch Dutton off guard as soon as I can. We've got the element of surprise on our side, so he won't know what hit him or what to do about it. And by the time he figures it out, it will be too late," Haggerty said.

"I hope so, Haggard. Let's get this over with as soon as possible, okay," Bellows demanded.

Haggerty reassured Bellows that everything would work out fine. He motioned to Jordan to head the cattle north. As the smaller herd moved out, Court Gary rode up alongside Bellows.

"So how many did you turn over to Haggard," Gary asked?

"Thirty percent like all the others. As you can see it's about seven hundred and fifty head. What about you," Bellows asked?

"Close to nine hundred; they took mine this morning," Gary replied.

"That herd he's planning on busting through the wire should be in the neighborhood of six thousand head. I hope he isn't planning on taking them and heading off to market them," Bellows reasoned.

"Don't worry about it, Royce; I've got men posted along the trail to the railhead just in case he tries something. He'll either deliver on what he has agreed to or we'll stretch his neck," Gary stated.

"I don't want any bloodshed over this mess, but it looks like Dutton is holding to his hard headedness. Why do some people have to be so gall darned ornery, Court," Bellows asked?

"Beats me...we sure aren't ornery, are we Royce," Gary grinned?

The two men laughed as the dust cloud created by the cattle shifted and began to cover them. Bellows and Gary reined their mounts around and rode away from the dust being kicked up by the cattle. Once away from the herd and the dust, Bellows looked back and then asked, "I've got a question for you Court?"

"Oh, what is it; I might know the answer?"

"Has Haggard let on where they are going to be keeping the cattle?"

"Nope, but I ain't worried about it. I don't think we'd have any trouble following the herd's trail; do you," Court said.

"No, I guess not. I was just wondering, that's all," Bellows answered.

Raymond D. Mason

10

Brian Sackett rode up to the wagon master's rig and stood up in the stirrups to stretch his back. He smiled at the wagon master and his wife and then said, "I thought this was all open range around here, Jed. Have you noticed all the barbed wire that's been strung?"

"I sure have, and I can guarantee you there are a lot of people upset by it. This land to the right of us belongs to George Dutton. It looks like he's going through with stringing that barbed wire. We heard about this all the way up in Sundown," Jed Corker said.

"I'd hate to get mixed up in a range war. I've seen all that kind of business I care to see for a long, long time," Brian said with a serious look on his face.

"Me too, Sackett; I guess we'll keep heading on farther south. This blasted dry spell is causing all kinds of havoc. How has it been where your spread is in Abilene?"

"A little better, but not much; we prepared for it and the smaller ranchers around us will have enough of our overflow to see them through this summer. Next year, though…well, let's just say I hope there comes some good rain storms between now and then. We may be facing the same situation that Dutton is facing out here," Brian said sounding almost apologetic.

The wagon master glanced back in the direction of the barbed wire and then saw two men riding along as though checking it. Brian noticed where the wagon train leader was looking and he too looked that way.

"They must be checking to make sure the wire got strung right," the wagon master stated.

"Yeah, I guess so," Brian said, just as AJ rode up to them.

"What is all this with the barbed wire," AJ asked?

"It's that George Dutton; he's the one stringing it. You said he was at our ranch nigh on to a year ago, didn't you, AJ," Brian said giving AJ a questioning look?

"Yep, nothing was said about barbed wire; not as I recall. He just wanted to buy some good horses. Of course, the dry conditions hadn't worsened then. I guess it's been a little drier in this area," AJ said giving the barbed wire a long look.

"You know some of the other ranchers won't take kindly to this," Brian offered.

"I wouldn't," AJ replied.

"Let's get back to the wagon and talk things over with Dan, Dean," AJ said, calling the twins by the names they'd given Corker.

The two rode back to Brent's wagon and swung around to ride alongside so they could talk.

Brian stated, "We've got a ways to go before we reach the cutoff to Abilene. We've been watching this barbed wire that's been strung and we sure don't want to get caught in a range war."

Brent nodded his head in agreement and said, "I've been watching it too. This was open range the last time I passed through here. You know this is going to bring about gunplay."

"Maybe we should cut cross country and take our chances making our own trail. If the shooting starts we don't want to be caught in the middle," Brian said thinking of Julia more than he and his brothers.

"No, I think we'd be safer staying with the other wagons for now. If we should get caught in crossfire we'd at least have plenty of guns helping us out," AJ said thoughtfully.

"I agree with AJ," Brent said. "I'll take care of Julia."

"Like you did when you got wounded," Brian replied?

Brent bristled slightly, "She didn't get hurt; I did."

"Don't get your dander up, Brent; I was just making an observation not a criticism," Brian said quickly.

Brent cooled down. He was touchy about his being seriously wounded while involved in a shootout that could have gotten both him and Julia killed. Still, he felt confident that it wouldn't happen again.

"You two knock it off. Julia will be safe as long as all three of us stick together. Just be ready for anything that might happen," AJ said evenly.

Haggerty and his men ran the last of the donated herds together with the others. It was getting late in the day and he didn't want to start the stampede towards the spot he'd picked until they'd started moving the cattle they planned on stealing towards the rail head.

"That's the last of them, Jack," Sterling called out to him.

"How many head did Conley donate," Haggerty called back?

"Eighteen hundred," Sterling replied.

"Cut two hundred and seventy out and put them in with the others we're holding aside," Haggerty answered.

"How many will that make," Sterling asked curiously?

"Nine hundred total. We should make out like 'bandits' on this deal," Haggerty said, getting a laugh from the men.

"What do you think we'll get a head," Sterling asked?

"I've already got a buyer and he's going twenty five dollars a head which brings the total to twenty two thousand, five hundred. Not bad for a shade over a weeks work, eh," Haggerty lied about the dollars per head he had lined up.

"Twenty two thousand and five hundred split how many ways, Jack," Sterling snapped?

"You have four men with you and Frank and I have three men with us. That makes ten men in all; so it would be two thousand two hundred and fifty dollars a piece. Why, Sam don't you trust me," Haggerty asked?

"No farther than I can throw my horse, Jack; you should know that," Sterling answered.

"Oh, you cut me to the quick, Sam. We'll all meet in Seminole after we've made the deal with the cattle buyer," Haggerty said.

"I'll go with you to seal the deal with the buyer. I wouldn't want you to get the idea to head off to Mexico without giving us our split," Sterling said.

"Oh, Sam, how could you even think such a thing," Haggerty feigned having his feelings hurt, which Sterling wasn't buying at all.

"Because I know you, Jack, remember that."

"Yeah, you can go along, but it will be up to you then to take the money back to your boys in Seminole. Frank and I will wash our hands of the whole deal between you and your boys. If you get the itch to take the money and ride hard and lonesome it will be between you and your boys; not us," Haggerty warned.

"They trust me, Jack; because they know they can," Sterling said with a frown.

Haggerty just smiled and slowly nodded his head. He'd worry about Sam Sterling when the time came. He knew one thing for sure, though; Sam's boys would get only what the ranchers paid them. As for Sam Sterling...he'd get a .44 slug in the heart.

PIMA COUNTY, ARIZONA

Buck Benton watched the lone rider coming down the hillside towards the ranch. He couldn't identify the man by the way he sat a horse, so figured the man must be a stranger.

The man was Clay Butler, and he was looking for work among other things. Clay had been on the trail of three men who'd robbed a Wells Fargo Bank in Cottonwood and had killed a teller while making their escape. The teller was his sister. Clay had been on their trail for over three weeks.

Clay rode up to where Buck was seated on the top rail of the corral fence and weaving a rawhide lariat. Clay tipped his hat as he rode up and stopped.

"Howdy," Clay said with a tight grin, "Do you do the hiring and firing around here?"

"I've been known to, yeah. Are you looking for work or a job," Buck asked?

Clay grinned at the question, "I'm looking for work and I'll do the best job for you that I can."

"That's what I wanted to hear. It just so happens I am looking to hire a good man. Do you have references," Buck asked?

"Not around here. I'm from up Cottonwood way. I have my own spread up there; a horse ranch; it's small, but it makes me a decent living. I'm down here on personal business and need to make my way seeing as how I'll be around here for awhile."

"I like your honesty. What kind of personal business are you on, if you don't mind my asking," Buck queried?

"I don't mind. I'm looking for three men that robbed a bank up in Cottonwood and shot and killed one of the tellers. She was my sister. I heard the men are from this area and I'm here to see justice done. If the law won't do anything to them, I will," Clay said evenly with a dead serious look.

Range War

"I see. How do you plan on working for us and looking for them at the same time? I'm looking for a cowhand, not a bounty hunter."

"I'm not a bounty hunter. I'll use my free time to find the men. If they're from around here they won't be hard to find. Meanwhile I have to eat and my money won't last me much longer. You won't regret hiring me, and that's a fact," Clay stated.

Buck looked him over and thought how much he reminded him of Linc Sackett. The two were about the same age and build and carried themselves well. He also noticed that Butler had his holster tied down; indicating he was probably fast on the draw. He liked what he saw in the man.

"What's your name," Buck asked?

"Clay Butler...and yours," Clay asked?

"Buck Benton, as you probably have already figured out, I'm the ranch foreman. You'll probably never meet the owner of the ranch. He lives back east and only gets out here about once a year and he just paid a visit a couple of months back. He pretty much leaves everything up to me. I like it like that and I guess he does too."

"You must be good at what you do," Clay said with a grin and a head nod.

"That I am! Stow your gear in the bunkhouse over there and come up to the big house and I'll get some information from you. I do have to keep some books on the running of the ranch," Buck chuckled.

"Thanks a lot, I really do appreciate this," Clay said.

"A good day's work is all I'm expecting out of you."

"You'll get it," Clay said and reined his horse in the direction of the bunkhouse.

Buck watched him for a few seconds and then climbed down off the corral fence and headed up to the ranch house. He wondered if Clay knew the names of the men he was looking for; if he did and they lived around the area, there was a good chance he'd know them.

11

LINC SACKETT walked into the bunkhouse after a long day of re-branding the cattle that Latimer and Haisley had tried to steal. He looked at the bunk that had been occupied by Jesse Latimer and saw that someone's gear was on it.

"Did we get a new hire," Linc asked?

"Looks that way, Linc," Shorty Alt said.

"Have you met him yet," Linc questioned?

"Nope; he's been up at the big house with Buck from what I heard. How's that branding going with those stolen cattle," Shorty asked?

"You make it sound like we stole 'em, Shorty," Linc laughed.

"Oh, you know what I mean, Linc."

"Yeah, I know. It's going okay. I'm putting our brand on the other side of their flank. There was too much done to the original brand so I'm just re-branding them."

Just then the door opened and Clay Butler walked in. He looked around at the half filled bunkhouse and tipped his hat towards the men.

"So you're the new hire, huh," Linc said with a friendly greeting?

"Yep, the name's Butler, Clay Butler."

"Nice to make your acquaintance, Clay; my name is Linc Sackett. Where do you hail from?"

"Cottonwood area; I actually have my own spread up that way, but I need work while I'm down here."

"I see. Well, welcome," Linc said with a slight wave.

The other men introduced themselves to Butler as well and he seemed to fit right in with them all. He was a likeable man of twenty eight years of age.

Buck Benton entered the bunkhouse and looked around at those present. He cleared his throat and got the men's attention.

"I take it you've all met our new hire, Clay Butler? If you haven't, then meet him now," Buck said.

"We've met him, Buck," Linc said with a grin.

"Good. Clay, I meant to ask you this earlier, but I forgot. It's about these men that you said killed your sister during the holdup. Do you happen to know any of their names," Buck asked?

There was a slight murmur raised when the men heard about his sister being killed.

Clay shook his head and said, "No, only that all three were riding horses with the same brand. One of the customers in the bank said he'd seen the brand when he passed through this area a few

Range War

months back. I figured they must be from around here and that's why I'm here."

"What was the brand; maybe we can help you out," Buck said.

"It was the Circle I-C brand," Clay said.

Buck looked quickly at Linc and then at the other men in the room. They all knew the brand. The brand belonged to Ike Carter. It was more than a mere possibility that some of Ike's men had robbed the bank up north. They were a bad lot. Clay noticed the looks that passed amongst the others.

"You've heard of that brand, haven't you," he said tightly.

Buck looked at him and then slowly nodded his head yes, "Yeah, we know the brand. It doesn't surprise us that some of their men might be involved in a bank job. The brand belongs to a man by the name of Ike Carter. He's bad and so are the men he hires."

"So what you're saying is that they won't be making a run for it any time soon," Clay said.

"Yep, I guess you could look at it that way," Buck answered.

"It'll take me a little while to determine who the men were who pulled off the robbery, but I will. Come Saturday night I'll start my inquiries into which of his men it might have been," Clay stated.

"Like I said, Clay, the Carter bunch is bad news. If you go after one, two, or three of their men you'll have the whole Carter payroll down on your neck. Of course, we'll back you if we can," Buck stated and then looked at the others. "I think so anyway."

87

"You'll have my support, Clay," Linc said quickly.

"Mine too," Shorty said.

"I'd like to help you out too, Clay," Jim Harris said.

Clay looked around the room at the guys he'd just met who were offering to stand with him. He nodded slowly and then stated. "If it comes to a showdown, I'll try and take the men one at a time, so hopefully I won't need your help. Thanks for offering; I really do appreciate it, but this is something I feel I have to do on my own."

"Clay, we've had run-ins with the Carter outfit before. It will be our pleasure to butt heads with them. They're a low down bunch of sidewinders who would just as soon bushwhack you as look at you. No, we'll be there, you can count on that," Buck quickly added.

Linc grinned as he surveyed the pearl handled pistol grip on Clay's pistol. Clay noticed and commented.

"Here, heft it," Clay said as he pulled the pistol out and handed it butt first to Linc.

"You don't mind?"

"No, I don't mind," Clay said with a slight grin and then added, "I couldn't help but notice yours, too. Mind if I try it?"

Buck saw that the two young men were wanting to test each other's prowess with a gun so he helped them out.

"I'll tell you boys what; let's go outside and you can try them out. Shorty, grab some cans and we'll set 'em on the corral fence posts," Buck said as the

Range War

men all began to grin at the thought of a shooting contest.

The bunkhouse emptied so they could all watch Linc and Clay show how good they were with shootin' irons. Shorty grabbed seven tin cans and ran up to the corral fence and placed them along the top rail.

More of the ranch hands were just getting in and saw right away what was about to take place. It wasn't long before a few bets were being placed on who the best man would be. They all knew how good Linc was with a gun, but Clay was a mystery to them.

"I've got a dollar and I'll take the new man," Jim Harris said.

"I'll cover that bet," Shorty said quickly.

After a few more bets were made, Buck told the two shooters to get ready.

"Okay, when I say 'go', Linc you start on the right side and work towards the middle. Clay, you work from the left to the middle. The first one to take the middle can is the winner," Buck said.

Linc gave a slight chuckle as did Clay. They looked at one another and Linc said, "I'll meet you in the middle."

The two men took a gunfighters stance and waited for the command to draw and start firing. Buck looked from one to the other and after a couple of silent seconds yelled, "Go."

Thunder rolled as the two men began firing in rapid succession. Cans on the right side went flying into the air, as did cans on the left side. Both men reached the middle can at the same time with Linc getting the first shot off.

The middle can went flying into the air, but hadn't even reached its peak when another shot rang out, sending the can even higher. It had come from Clay's gun. Before the can hit the ground Linc fired and kicked it up into the air again, where Clay fired and sent it higher.

Linc didn't fire again, which allowed the can to hit the ground. Everyone was whooping and hollering. Clay looked at Linc and grinned before saying, "You keep the hammer on an empty chamber don't you."

"Yep, only five slugs," Linc smiled.

"Same here," Clay said and he too smiled.

Buck laughed as he declared, "I call it a draw. Man, can you guys shoot. I pity anyone who gets in a shootout with either one of you."

A new friendship was born at that moment between Linc Sackett and Clay Butler. It was a friendship that would last for over fifteen years and right up until the death of one of the two men.

12

Black Jack Haggerty sat watching the men riding guard along the line of barbed wire at the spot he'd chosen to stampede the cattle through. While he was here to make sure that the break through went off without a hitch, Frank Jordan was busy moving close to nine hundred head of cattle in the direction of the railhead.

There was a cloud cover and only a quarter moon shining so the midnight hour was shrouded in darkness. This was just what Haggerty had hoped for; deep darkness. He had a buyer waiting at the railhead in Lamesa ready to pay him thirty dollars a head with no questions asked.

Jordan moved the cattle at a fast pace in order to get them to the waiting cattle cars before sunup. Haggerty waited until Sterling's men had passed one another and then gave the order to stampede the herd of over five thousand head of cattle.

The cattle had been held far enough away that their lowing could not be heard by the men on the barbed wire line. Haggerty had chosen the spot for the stampede carefully and had planned on using a narrow draw for the cattle to stampede down to the wire through.

When the first shots rang out the cattle bolted and headed towards the draw. The gunshots were heard by the men riding guard on the fence line and they prepared for a shootout. They had not prepared for a stampede.

When the men riding sentry duty along the wire first heard and then saw the stampeding herd, they immediately began firing to try and divert the charging cattle. It didn't work because of the narrow draw the cattle were encased in.

Whooping, hollering and waving burlap sacks Haggerty's men charged the herd towards the wire. The lead cattle burst through the wire and a number of cattle went down. The trailing cattle either went around the downed cattle, or jumped over them, or trampled them. Needless to say the wire at that particular point was broken and a tangled mess.

Once the cattle had gotten through the wire Haggerty's men concentrated on Sterling's men and the shooting became directed at them. Men from both sides fell to the ground; some wounded and some dead. Haggerty, however, peeled off and was never in danger of getting hit by a stray bullet.

Seeing that the cattle had accomplished what he'd planned, Haggerty reined his horse in the direction of the railhead. He wanted to meet up with Jordan and be there to settle up with the cattle buyer himself.

Range War

    The spot that Haggerty had chosen to break through the wire was only about a half mile from a good sized watering hole, so the cattle headed straight for it. He knew that this would keep both sides in the range war busy for hours.

    What Haggerty had not planned on, however, was the fact that Court Gary had assigned a man by the name of Bales to keep close tabs on him. As soon as Bales saw Haggerty leave the stamped and head out to find Jordan he followed him. When Bales saw Haggerty heading towards the railhead, he knew something was up.

    Another man had also been keeping a close eye on Haggerty; Sam Sterling. As soon as he saw the stampeding cattle he began to look for Haggerty figuring he would not put himself in danger. Once he spotted Haggerty leaving the scene, he also followed him to see where he was heading.

    Bales kept a close eye on Haggerty and once he saw the herd that Jordan was taking to the railhead turned around and headed for the Gary ranch. He hadn't gone far when he ran headlong into Sterling. Bales didn't recognize Sterling and thought he worked for the ranchers who were opposed to the barbed wire.

    "Haggard has stolen hundreds of cattle and is driving them towards the railhead," Bales said.

    "Is that right," Sterling said as he rode up alongside Bales. "Well, imagine that."

    Before Bales knew what was happening Sterling pulled a hunting knife from his boot top and shoved it between his ribs. Bales fell out of the saddle, mortally wounded. Sterling looked down at him for a moment and then reined his horse around and continued his pursuit of Haggerty.

The nine hundred head of cattle that Jordan was driving to the railhead began to spread out due to not enough drovers being used. Jordan was certainly no working cowboy. He'd never done anymore than steal cattle and usually the rest of the gang would be the ones controlling the herd.

"Frank, these cattle are scattering all over the country side," one of the men yelled.

"I can't help it; just do the best you can. We've got to get as many as we can to the railhead before sun-up. Stampede 'em if you have to," Jordan yelled back.

"Haggerty ain't going to like that," the man replied.

"Just do as you're told. They won't scatter as much if they're running full out."

"Okay...come on men, stampede 'em," the man yelled out.

Haggerty's men began whooping and hollering and spooking the cattle. They began to run straight ahead which was heading them in the direction of the trail the small wagon train was on that included the Sackett boys.

Haggerty was close enough to the herd to know there was a second stampede from all the noise. He clenched his teeth in anger as he thought of Jordan stampeding the herd; and for the life of him could not understand why he would to it.

Brent was the first to hear the approaching cattle and sat upright in bed. He looked around to get a fix on the direction from which the sound was

Range War

coming. He leaped out of the bed in the wagon and down to the ground.

By this time Brian and AJ, who had been bedded down beneath the wagon, were awake as well. They all three looked in the direction that the sound was coming from.

"Stampede," AJ said.

"Quick, get under the wagon," Brent said and climbed back into the wagon and grabbed Julia. He literally tossed her to the waiting arms of his two brothers who caught her and shoved her under the wagon.

"As soon as we see them start firing your gun into the air to turn them away from us," AJ said.

"Shoot the lead steers," Brent said. "That'll help turn the others as well."

Brian untied the saddle horses in order to give them a chance to get away from the thundering herd. Of course, they had no way of knowing how many head of cattle were on the move, but expected a large herd.

Just before the herd arrived at the campsite of the small wagon train, the sliver of a moon broke through the thin cloud cover and gave them a little better lighting. Shortly after that the herd made its appearance, also.

"Now," AJ yelled out and began firing his pistol at the lead steers.

Brian and Brent did the same thing. Frank Jordan heard the gunshots but couldn't see who was doing the firing. When he saw the wagons he realized that the people in them were killing the lead cattle.

Jordan began firing at the wagons in an effort to silence their guns. He rode close enough to Brent's wagon that Brent got a fairly good look at Jordan's face. Brent raised his rifle and aimed it at the approaching Jordan.

When the gun bucked in Brent's hand, Jordan did a somersault off the back of his horse when the slug from the Winchester '73 hit him in the chest. Frank 'Four Fingers' Jordan was dead.

The cattle somehow missed the wagon that Julia and the boys were hiding under. A couple of the other wagons weren't so lucky, although no one was seriously hurt. Even the Sackett's horses were easily rounded up.

Haggerty had finally caught up with what remained of the stolen cattle and was livid. There were no more than a couple of hundred head left with most of the others scattered over the range land. He became even angrier when he learned that Frank Jordan had been killed during the stampede. He didn't know who the man was who had killed his old friend and partner and really didn't care.

"How did this happen," Haggerty fumed?

"It was Jordan's doing. The cattle started drifting all over the place and Jordan told us to stampede the herd to get them to run in a more straight line. That man sure wasn't no cattle man, I can tell you that," Haggerty's man told him.

"That idiot; I knew I should have let someone else take care of the moving of the herd. Well, round up what you can and let's get them on to the railhead. How many do you think we still have," Haggerty asked?

"I'd say maybe three hundred, no more than three fifty," the man said.

From behind Haggerty, Sterling's voice boomed, "And those will be split up evenly with the boys left alive."

Haggerty spun around in the saddle and his hand moved like lightning towards his gun. As he drew the gun from its holster he cocked the hammer back and fired all in one move. The bullet hit Sterling in the neck, knocking him from the saddle.

Sterling's foot caught in the stirrup and the horse bolted. It took off in a full out run down the trail dragging the half dead Sterling along the ground. With his boot hung in the stirrup and his wound so severe, Sterling was helpless. The horse ran for a good hundred yards before slowly coming to a halt.

Sterling lay with his boot still caught in the stirrup. He didn't move. It was obvious that Sam Sterling was dead. The man with Haggerty looked on in stunned silence. He'd heard that Haggerty was a hard man and this proved it.

"Come on, we've got work to do," Haggerty snapped.

Raymond D. Mason

13

COURT GARY looked down at the dead body of his friend, Bales. He shook his head as he clenched his teeth in silent anger. He knew who had done this; at least he thought he knew. It had to be either 'Haggard' or one of Haggard's men.

"We shouldn't have any trouble following the herd," Gary said.

"I don't know boss," one of the men who worked for him said. "These guys didn't know the first thing about herding cattle. There're cattle scattered all over the place. It will take us a couple of days to get them all rounded up and into one herd."

"They had to be driving these cattle to the railhead. Obviously they didn't make it. You men start rounding the cattle up and I'll ride on and see if I can pick up another trail," Gary stated.

Gary kicked his horse up and soon was able to pick up the trail of the cattle that had met up with the small wagon train. When he saw the cleanup that was taking place he knew he was on the right track.

Gary rode up to the first wagon he came to which was Brent's. He looked around at the dead cattle they had been forced to shoot and shook his head.

"Were these your cattle," Brent asked, getting Gary's attention?

Gary gave Brent a quick look and answered, "Yes, some of them were mine and a number of other rancher's as well. We had a man try and steal them from us."

Brent walked over to where he'd dragged Frank Jordan's body and asked, "Was this man with the one who tried to steal the cattle?"

Gary looked closely at Jordan and nodded his head yes, "Yeah, he sure was. The other man's name is Haggard."

"Well, you're partly right; his name is actually Haggerty; as in Black Jack Haggerty. This is Frank 'Four Fingers' Jordan," Brent said looking down at the dead man. "How'd they come to steal your cattle, anyway?"

"You wouldn't believe me if I told you; heck, I don't even believe it. We paid them to steal them although we didn't know we were doing it at the time," Gary stated.

"You're right...I don't get it?"

"We hired him to fight a range war for us. Does that explain it any better? Of course, we didn't know we were hiring Black Jack Haggerty when we did it."

"You folks must really be removed from any news out this way. His likeness has been on wanted posters all over the state. And how could you have missed 'Four Fingers' Jordan," Brent said with a slight frown as he bent down and held up Jordan's hand with fingers missing?

"You know, he kept a glove on his hand most of the time, so we never even noticed. He won't be giving any one any trouble from now on," Gary stated.

"So you say you're on the trail of Haggerty," Brent asked?

"Yeah, it looks to me like he's trying to get some of our cattle to the railhead. I'm hoping to catch him before he can secure a deal, or get the cattle loaded onto cattle cars."

"I'm not going to ask the particulars, I'll just say I hope you catch him. When you do, do the entire human race a big favor and shoot the man dead," Brent said seriously.

"I feel like it, believe me. Sorry about all this. None of your people were hurt, I hope," Gary said sincerely.

"No, we managed to be spared," Brent came back.

"Good! Adios, my friend," Gary said.

Court looked at the dead steers as he rode on in the direction of the railhead. Brent saw him shake his head as he looked at the destruction; both the dead cattle and the strewn goods of the one's who'd had their wagons destroyed.

Brian and AJ had gone to fetch their horses and were just coming back into camp as Court was leaving. They rode up to where Brent was and AJ asked, "Who was that?"

"One of the ranchers who had some of these cattle stolen from them. And you'll never guess who stole them," Brent said with a grin.

"Black Jack Haggerty," Brian said.

Brent looked funny, "How'd you know that?"

Brian laughed as he said, "You killed Four Fingers Jordan last night and you ask who stole the cattle? Those two go together like biscuits and gravy. Wherever you find one you find the other."

Brent chuckled, "Oh, yeah, I guess that does make sense. Anyway, the ranchers involved in the range war actually hired Haggerty to help them fight Dutton. He saw an opportunity to steal a number of cattle from them and took it. They must have stampeded and this is the result."

"We're only one mile from the trail to Abilene," AJ cut in. "Let's get everything ready and head on home."

They had just started to load their belongings into the wagon when three more men rode up. The men stopped and looked around at the dead cattle's dead carcasses.

"Did you kill these cattle," the older man asked with a frown?

"Some of them," AJ answered with a slight scowl on his face. "Why do you ask?"

"Some of these were my steers," the man said.

"You're one of the ranchers that threw in with the man who just left here, I guess," Brent stated.

"Oh, and who was that?"

"He didn't give me a name and I didn't ask. He said he was on the trail of a man he knew as Haggard who in reality is Black Jack Haggerty," Brent replied.

Range War

The three men looked at one another somewhat wide eyed. "Did you say 'Black' Jack Haggerty," one of the men asked?

Brent nodded his head, "I did," he said.

"Which way did he go," the older man asked?

"Towards the railhead; he said he wanted to catch up to Haggerty. If the man is a friend of yours, you'd better give him a hand because he's going to need your help," Brent said evenly.

"Yeah, I can see that. Thanks," the older man said.

The Sackett's watched as the men kicked up their horses and headed in the direction of the railhead. Brent shook his head slowly as he watched the men ride away.

"What is it, Brent," AJ asked?

"Haggerty is the one who almost killed me. Maybe I ought to go and give those guys a hand," Brent said seriously.

"Oh, no you don't," Julia's voice said coming from behind the three brothers. "I just got you healed up from your last encounter with that man and I'm not taking any chances on losing you again."

Brent couldn't hold back the chuckle as he turned and looked at the love of his life. She walked up and put her arm around Brent's waist as if to show the world that she wasn't about to let him go off and maybe get himself killed.

"Okay, you win," Brent said. "Let's get on our way to Abilene."

Haggerty took a more direct route to the railhead and had already arrived there by the time the sun came up. The cattle buyer was disappointed at the small size of the herd, but paid Haggerty the same price he'd agreed on which was thirty dollars a head; five dollars more than what Haggerty had been telling his men the man would pay.

"Here you go, Mr. Haggard...nine thousand five hundred and seventy dollars," the cattle buyer said as he counted out the money to Jack.

"Thank you, Drake; I'm sorry I couldn't deliver all the cattle I said I would. Stampedes happen though. This one was costly," Haggerty said as he shoved the money under his shirt.

"I hope you're not planning on walking around like that," Mr. Drake said.

"It's safer there than it is in any bank I've ever been in," Haggerty grinned.

"Well, good day. Now that we've counted the cattle we'll start loading them into the cattle cars. Nice doing business with you Mr. Haggard," Drake said.

"Yeah, Drake; and back at you. Well, adios Amigo," Haggerty said as he turned and walked out of Drake's small office inside the train station.

Haggerty was still angry about the loss of all the cattle, but at least he had close to ten thousand dollars and was only going to give the men with him five hundred each. His share of the money would be well over six thousand dollars.

"Come on men, let's head for Big Spring. I don't want to be hanging around here for long," Haggerty said when he faced the men waiting for him outside Drake's office.

Range War

"Just give us our money now, Jack. I'm on my way to San Antone," one of the men said.

"Okay, if that's the way you want it," Haggerty said and counted out five hundred to the man.

"I was thinking more like a thousand," the man said with a scowl.

"I was thinking a lot more cattle, Big Ear," Haggerty snapped angrily.

"Well, five hundred is better than wages. Adios," Big Ear said as he took the money and mounted his horse.

"Well, I may as well pay all of you. Here," Haggerty said as he began paying off the men.

Each man took his five hundred and gave Haggerty a dirty look. They knew that his take had to be several thousand. They didn't like it, but felt helpless at doing anything about it, seeing as how he set everything up. Besides, they knew how the man was when they agreed to coming along on this venture.

Haggerty had just paid the last man off when the county sheriff suddenly appeared on the scene. He gave Haggerty and the other two men who where still with him a hard gaze.

"You wouldn't be Haggard, would you," the sheriff asked?

Haggerty knew that the only ones calling him by Haggard were the ones involved in the range war. He had to think fast.

"No, my name is Spencer. Why do you ask, Sheriff," Haggerty lied?

"I just had a visit from a man giving me a description that fits you to a T. Only he said the

105

man fitting that description's name would be Haggard."

"You've got the wrong man," Haggerty said as he slowly moved towards his horse.

"Why don't you come along with me and we'll wait for the man to come and identify you one way or the other," the sheriff said resting his hand on his pistol grip.

"Sure, Sheriff, just let me get something out of my saddlebag," Haggerty said and turned his back to the sheriff.

When Haggerty turned back around to face the sheriff he was holding a six shooter and shot the sheriff in the chest. The sheriff fell to the ground and Haggerty swung into the saddle. He cast a quick look at the sheriff as he and the others kicked their horses into a full run away from the small depot.

14

HAGGERTY YELLED OUT, "Split up. They can't follow all of us."

He headed off by himself figuring to head south before cutting towards the west. He'd head for Arizona now. He certainly couldn't remain in these parts. It would be odd not having Frank Jordan with him; they had ridden together for almost ten years.

Haggerty rode his horse hard, putting as much distance as he could between himself and the ranchers he'd swindled. He knew they would have riders out looking for him as well as the law. He knew also, that his best bet was to head for open range and avoid as many towns as he could for awhile.

Here he had thousands of dollars stuffed in his shirt and no where to spend it. He was sick of Mexico and the only place he figured he'd be safe until the heat died down was Arizona Territory.

Having traveled a good ten miles from Lamesa Haggerty's horse came up lame. It began to favor its right front leg causing him to stop and check to see what the problem was. He raised its hoof and saw nothing out of the ordinary. Running his hand along its foreleg he realized that the horse had possibly pulled a ligament.

This horse would be no good to him now. He'd have to find another mount; but, where? He unsaddled the animal and slung the saddle and bridle over his shoulder while he carried his rifle and saddlebags in the other hand. Noticing a thin trail of smoke coming from over a distant hilltop, he headed in its direction.

Haggerty knew he had to find a good horse, and soon, if he was going to get away from those he knew would be pursuing him. He hoped the smoke was coming from a homesteader's place that might have a good horse he could buy, or steal; he didn't care which.

Meanwhile, the ranchers and their cowhands had arrived at the railhead and found out that Haggerty had already been there and was gone. The sheriff had died and a telegram had been sent to a federal marshal; a man by the name of John Bridger. Also the Texas Rangers had been alerted and were on the lookout for Black Jack Haggerty as well.

George Dutton surveyed the damage his barbed wire fence had suffered due to the stampede and shook his head. Four of his men had been killed and two others wounded during the stampede.

Sterling was dead and he didn't know who to blame or credit for that killing.

From where the breakthrough had occurred, Dutton rode along the trail the stampeding cattle had taken and it led him straight to one of his watering holes. Just about all the cattle were gathered around the water, with some even standing knee deep out in it.

This whole thing had gotten out of hand and he wasn't happy about it. Dutton had not changed his mind one bit about keeping the other ranchers off his range, and this incident only added fuel to the range war fire. Someone had to pay for this, but who; Court Gary, or maybe Royce Bellows?

"Jeff," Dutton called out to one of his hired hands, "Get some of the other men to help you and start rounding up these cattle and getting them back on the other side of the fence line. The barbed wire stays! We'll restring the wire that was ripped out. This one incident isn't going to change a thing. They've forced my hand now and I'll not give in to their demands."

"What do you want me to do with the cattle once their on the other side of the wire, boss?"

"Leave 'em. Let the ranchers that own them deal with 'em," Dutton snapped.

Dutton kicked up his horse and headed for the railhead. He had some telegrams to send off and wanted to get it done quickly. If the other ranchers were going to play rough, so was he. He'd bring in enough 'Regulators' to squash any attempt to cross his property line.

PIMA COUNTY, ARIZONA

Raymond D. Mason

IKE CARTER'S RANCH

Ike Carter looked across the table at Johnny Rio. Rio had gone to work for him a few months earlier and was hired for one reason and one reason only; his gun. Carter wanted men working his ranch that knew how to handle a gun because of past run-ins with other ranchers and the law.

"What is this I hear about some of the boys robbing a bank up in Cottonwood, Johnny; do you know anything about it," Ike asked?

"I've heard a few rumors, but I don't know all that much about it. Why do you ask?"

"I got word from the territorial marshal that our brand was on the horses used in the holdup. I want to know who it was that held up that bank. I'll send them to my cousin's place in Waco. I don't want them bringing the law down on us; we've got enough trouble as it is," Ike explained.

"What if they don't want to go to Waco," Rio asked?

"Then they're on their own, but they'll be on their own without our horses being involved. I don't want that identity tied to their doings."

"I'll put the word out and see if I can learn who the three men were," Rio said.

"Let me know as soon as you find out," Ike said and then added. "The marshal told me that a woman was killed during the holdup and she might have a brother looking for the men. I don't know his name, but the marshal said he'd let me know if he learns the man's moniker."

Range War

"That's not the reason you want to send the one's responsible to Waco is it, Ike; because of one man," Rio questioned with a frown?

"No, no, I just don't want the law snooping around here. I don't worry about the territorial marshal; I've got him in my pocket. There's another one down here that I don't want snooping around though; that's Bud Starr," Ike said.

"He must be a new one; I don't think I've heard of him," Rio stated.

"He was the sheriff up in Laramie, but he and his wife moved down here to Arizona and now he's been made a territorial marshal. He's a tough one, I can tell you that," Ike replied.

"They're all just men. They cut, bleed, and die just like everyone else," Rio said.

"Yeah, but some don't cut as easy, they don't bleed as much, and they're harder to kill," Ike said, getting in the last word.

Rio walked to the door and looked back, "I'll let you know what I find out about the bank holdup, Ike."

With that Rio walked out and headed towards the bunkhouse. Ike continued to stare at the door for several seconds and then said aloud, "You find 'em for me, Rio and I'll see to it that they're not heard of again."

Linc Sackett and Clay Butler rode up a draw and spotted a couple of stray steers. They circled the cattle and headed them back down the draw towards the main herd. Clay had been in deep thought and Linc had noticed.

"What's eatin' at you, Clay," Linc asked?

"I'm no closer to finding out who killed my sister, Linc," Butler replied.

"You said they were riding horses that wore the Circle I-C brand, let's ride over there and ask around. We'll take a couple of the other boys with us," Linc suggested.

"If we do that, we alert them to the fact that someone is looking for them. I figure the first night I have off and go into the cantina I'll have a better chance of finding out their names," Butler said thoughtfully.

"You have a point there. There ain't much in the way of a town, as towns go. It has one saloon though; Muldoon's. We'll go in Saturday night and ask around," Linc said.

Clay smiled and nodded as he said, "You're a good man, Linc. I'm truly glad I made your acquaintance. I hope we can always remain friends."

"I don't see why we wouldn't...do you," Linc grinned?

"Nope...not at all," Clay agreed.

15

Black Jack Haggerty knelt down behind a small tree and watched the homesteader's house to see if he could determine how many people were around. He could see a wash hanging on the line and could make out some men's clothes and a couple of shirts that might be either a young boy's or a woman's. He also saw a pair of Levis that were larger than the other pair.

Haggerty eyed the saddle resting on the small corral rail fence next to the barn. He grinned sensing that there would be at least one decent saddle horse at his disposal. He had just started to move in towards the house when a woman walked out of the house and started towards the clothes line.

Jack stopped short, holding his position, as the woman began checking the clothes to see if they were dry. Some of the thinner garments she took down, but left the heavier things signifying they had not yet dried.

As she started back towards the house with an armload of clothes, movement in back of her caused her to turn and look towards it. Haggerty was surprised when she suddenly dropped the clothes she was carrying and started running towards the house.

Six Kiowa Indians suddenly appeared on horseback no more than twenty yards from the barn. The woman made it to the house just as the first Kiowa warrior threw his lance and stuck it in the door as she closed it.

Haggerty hoisted his rifle to his shoulder ready to start firing at the marauding Indians, but held off. The thought ran through his mind that the Indians might give him a better chance to get himself a horse. He'd wait it out and see what developed.

The Indians circled the house while the woman pulled a Sharps buffalo rifle down from where it hung over the door. She ran to a window and aimed at the Indians, but didn't fire. Haggerty watched in silence.

Finally the woman fired the Sharps, but the bullet flew harmlessly wide of its mark. She quickly reloaded the single shot rifle and fired again; and again missed whatever it was she was shooting at. Her firing didn't go unnoticed, however.

About a half mile away her husband and his brother were busy trying to pull a stump out of the ground when they heard the first shot. With the wooded area between them and the house they had not been able to see the small war party, but they certainly heard the roar of the Sharps.

Range War

As soon as they heard the first shot they scrambled aboard their horses and made a mad dash towards the house. This told Haggerty all he needed to know about the occupants; especially when he looked towards the barn and saw a boy and girl look out at the Kiowa and then duck back inside the barn.

If Haggerty had one soft spot it was definitely towards children; at least those under the age of twelve. He'd lost a brother and a sister of eight and nine when he was just a boy himself and had always had a special feeling for the young.

Seeing one of the Kiowa warriors looking in the direction of the barn alerted Haggerty to the fact that the brave might have seen the kids. He watched closely as the brave reined his horse in the direction of the barn and leaped to the ground when he drew near the front door.

Haggerty raised the rifle once again and took aim at the warrior. He was just about to squeeze off a round when the arrival of the woman's husband and his brother occurred.

The Kiowa war party turned their attention towards the two men who were firing their six guns. They weren't the best of shots, but at least they were able to distract the marauding Indians.

Haggerty took this opportunity to pick off a couple of Kiowa warriors. The first one was the brave nearest the barn where the kids were. The bullet hit him between the shoulder blades.

One of the braves still on horseback saw where the rifle fire had come from and rode towards Haggerty's position. He was only about twenty feet from Haggerty when a bullet from the bad man's rifle knocked him off his horse backwards.

With only four warriors remaining, the war party quickly gave up their attack. They rode hard back into the gulley from which they'd come. Haggerty stepped out into the open once the Kiowa had gone.

Holding his rifle above his head to show he meant them no harm, Haggerty started walking towards the house. The two men went to meet him; both wearing big smiles.

"Man, are we glad you showed up. Do you think they might come back," one of the men asked?

"I'd say so; but only after they join the larger party that I ran across about three miles back. They caught up to me about a mile from here and shot my horse out from under me, but I managed to lose them and when I saw the smoke from your smoke stack I headed this way. I guess they saw the smoke too," Haggerty lied.

"How big a war party was it," the woman's husband asked?

"At the time I thought it must be at least a hundred, but looking back on it now I'd say no more than forty, maybe forty five," Haggerty continued with his lie.

"We can't hold out against a war party that size. If those Indians were on their way to join up with the larger war party that would make it around fifty! Do you think we ought to make a run for it," the husband asked?

"All of us wouldn't stand a chance. They'd catch us out in open country and that would be all

Range War

she wrote. No, it would be better if one man tried to get help. How far is it to the nearest town, anyway," Haggerty asked?

"About six miles to the town of Bolton; and that would be as the crow flies. By the road it would be closer to eight, nine miles," the husband stated.

"How many guns do you have here on your place," Haggerty questioned?

"These two pistols we're carrying and a Sharps rifle inside the house."

"That's all? Man, you wouldn't stand a chance against a large raiding party. I'll tell you what I'll do. I'll leave my Winchester with you and that will give you a repeater as well as what you already have. I'll go for help and lead them back here. Which of these two horses is the fastest," Haggerty went on with his lie?

"This one," the husband said. "Do you have any extra cartridges for that Winchester," the man asked?

"I've got a full box in my saddlebags. I'll get it and leave it with you. I'd better get a move on though. Get that saddle off your horse; I managed to get mine off my horse once the raiding party had passed by where I had hid from them," Haggerty stated, thinking quickly.

"Yeah, sure...Billy, you keep a sharp eye out to make sure the raiding party doesn't come back," the husband said to his younger brother.

Haggerty hurriedly ran to where he had left his saddle and carried it over to the unsaddled horse. He pretended to be concerned about the Kiowa returning, but in reality was concerned about the rancher's men who might have picked up his trail.

"What's your name, Mister," the husband asked as Haggerty threw his saddle on the horse?

"Haggard," Haggerty said. "Which is the best way to cut cross country to town from here," he asked?

"Head for that hill over yonder and go right over the top of it; you'll see the road down below you," the husband said taking a quick look towards the dry wash that the Kiowa had made their escape down.

"I'll be back as soon as possible with as many men as I can muster. We'll go after that bunch and the one's they joined up with," Haggerty said exaggerating his concern.

"Oh, here are the extra cartridges for that Winchester. Take care of it; that's the best rifle I've ever owned," Haggerty then added.

The homesteader nodded and smiled as he said, "God speed."

"God speed," Haggerty answered and kicked the horse up.

Haggerty had no intention of going for help; he had the horse he needed to make good his escape from his pursuers. He headed in the direction the homesteader had pointed and once he topped the hilltop saw the road below him.

"Next stop, Bolton," Haggerty said with a wide grin. "And from there it's on to Arizona."

Range War

16

CARTER RANCH, ARIZONA

JOHNNY RIO pointed towards three men just riding up to the bunkhouse and said to Ike Carter, "That's the ones who robbed the bank in Cottonwood; Luther King, Bill Leonard, and Jim Crane."

"I figured it was those three. I'll have to get them off the ranch and quick. I can't have that marshal poking around here. I heard he was at Camp Thomas yesterday. I'm sure he'll be making his way to this area," Ike said with a frown.

"Go tell them I want to see them up at the house," Ike added.

"Okay...are you going to fire them," Johnny asked?

"No, I'll just have them lay low for awhile. Like I said, if they want to work they can go to Waco and I'll wire my cousin and tell him to give them a job," Ike said.

Range War

"Okay, I'll tell them," Rio said and headed in the direction of the bunkhouse.

The three men knocked on the front door of the ranch house and Ike yelled for them to come in. They went in with their hats in their hands and a worried look on their faces.

"I hear you boys robbed a bank up in Cottonwood; is that right," Ike started the conversation.

The three cast a quick look amongst themselves and then at Ike.

"Who told you that," Luther King asked?

"Never mind who; I know you did and that's all that you need to be concerned with. I just wish you wouldn't ride horses that carry my brand on 'em," Ike said with a deep frown.

The three looked quickly at one another again and Jim Crane said, "Ike we hadn't really planned on robbing that bank. You had sent us up there to check on some cattle and the bank looked so ripe for picking that we just couldn't help ourselves."

"Yeah, well you killed someone during that holdup and I hear there's a territorial marshal down here looking for you. I want you boys to get out of here until the heat dies down. Now I've been checking around and you can go one of two places.

"You can either go to a cousin of mine back in Waco, Texas, or you can head down closer to the border to a friend of mine down there; Old Man Clanton. You can help him run cattle from Mexico across the border to his ranch until I send for you. The choice is up to you," Ike said.

"Old Man Clanton is my choice," King said, getting agreeing nods from the other two as well.

"Okay, that settles it. You boys head on down to his ranch near Camp Thomas in the Gila River Valley area. Just tell him I sent you and he'll find something for you to do. I'll get in touch with you when it's safe to come back here," Carter stated.

Without another word the men turned and walked out of the house and down to the bunkhouse to get their belongings. Within five minutes they were in the saddle and on the move to Old Man Clanton's spread.

Ike Carter wasn't upset that some of his men had robbed a bank. He just didn't want them using his horses when doing it. He'd prefer they steal some horses to be used in holdups.

ABILENE, TEXAS
THE SACKETT RANCH

John Sackett walked out onto the front porch of the Sackett ranch house and looked down the long lane that led to the house from the main road. He recognized the two riders instantly as US Marshal Ben Coyle and Martin Bloom his deputy.

They climbed off their mounts and tied them to the hitching rail with John watching them the entire time. When they got within earshot the marshal greeted John, who nodded slightly.

"We came to see if you'd heard anything from your two sons. We heard they were in town and stocked up on some supplies. Were they taking a little trip," the marshal asked with a serious look on his face.

"That's pretty obvious, Marshal. Yeah, I had them going to check on some cattle I'm interested

Range War

in buying," John said stretching the truth considerably.

"During a long dry spell; somehow I doubt that, John," the marshal said.

"The dry spell won't last forever."

"I've received word that your sons were seen up near Lubbock County," the marshal said inquisitively.

"If you knew that, why'd you ask me if they'd taken a trip? You already knew they had," John said tightly.

"I just wanted to see if you'd lie for them. Who'd they go to see in Lubbock County?"

"You know so much...you tell me," John replied steely eyed.

"I'm going to find Brent and when I do I'm taking him in; one way or another I'm taking him in. It will go a lot easier on you if you don't try and hide him out. I'm asking you to tell me what you know about his whereabouts," Marshal Coyle said.

"No, what you're asking me to do is help you slip a noose around my son's neck. I'm not going to help you find him, so you can grind that up, stuff it in your pipe and smoke it. Now, I've said all I'm going to say on this subject. Was there something else you wanted to talk to me about," John said firmly?

"No, I've said what I came to say. But, if your boys show up here and Brent's with them, I'll consider them to be the Sackett Gang, and I'll take 'em all three in."

"Get off my land," John said tightly.

"We'll go; but we'll be back and when we come there won't just be two of us. It will be a forty man posse, you can count on it."

"You know what you can do with your forty man posse and the horses they'd be riding...now git," John snapped.

The marshal and his deputy climbed back on their horses and headed towards the main road with John staring hard at their backs. He wasn't about to turn Brent over to the marshal and he would gladly face the consequences.

As John stood there he suddenly had a thought that caused him to tense up. What if the boys came through Abilene on their way to the ranch? The marshal would have them arrested before they got a mile out of town. He wished he knew where they were so he could send someone to warn them.

Quickly John went to the corral and saddled his horse. He rode out to where he had some of his cowhands branding yearlings and when he saw Jake Hardin called him over to him.

"Jake, I want you do something that might be danged near impossible," John stated.

"Oh, what's that, boss?"

"I want you to take some supplies and go and see if you can locate AJ and Brian. I know it's like asking you to find a needle in a haystack, but you've got to do it if you can. If you find 'em, tell them to swing wide of Abilene on their way back to the ranch.

"If they have Brent with them tell them they'd better be doubly careful. The US Marshal Ben Coyle is waiting for them to show up around town and if Brent's with them he's going to arrest all three of them.

"Coyle just told me that they'd been spotted up in Lubbock County, so start for there and maybe you'll meet them on the way. If not...well, just ask around and see if anyone remembers seeing them. Like I said, I know it's an impossible task, but you've got to do your best," John said.

"I'll do the best I can, boss; you can be sure of that. We ran across a drifter the other day and he said he'd heard there was Comanche trouble up in the Lubbock County area," Jake said.

"Is that right," John said thoughtfully. He paused for a moment and then added, "Pick someone to go with you; just to be on the safe side."

"Can I take Lee Goodnight," Jake asked?

"He'd be a good choice; especially the way he can handle a rifle; sure, take Lee with you," John said.

John knew that what he was asking was more wishful thinking than anything, but he had to try and get word to his sons.

The last thing he wanted was to see any of them arrested or worse yet, hanged. AJ and Brian hadn't done anything to be hanged for on their own; but aiding Brent would put them at odds with the law; especially from what Brian had said about Brent's troubles. You could be sure a noose was waiting for him.

Raymond D. Mason

17

BRIAN AND AJ SACKETT reined their horses to a stop and looked out over the watering hole known as Big Springs. There was nothing there at the time, but the spot was a favorite watering hole for anyone traveling the trail that let by here. It was also a spot the Comanche and Pawnee visited on a regular basis.

"Do you see any Indian sign," Brian asked AJ?

"Nope...the only thing I see is a small wagon train headed this way. Look back yonder," AJ said pointing to the east.

"Yeah, I see them. We can ask them if they've encountered any trouble along the way. I hope not; I don't want to see another Indian or a steer until we get to the ranch," Brian said with a laugh.

"You and me both," AJ said and then looked back at the wagon with Brent driving and Julia seated next to him.

"Brent looks happier than I can remember, doesn't he," AJ commented.

"Yeah, it looks like his love for Julia has soothed the hard feelings he had towards us. Now that's the kind of woman you need, AJ; one who has eyes for one man and one man only," Brian said with a wry grin.

"They don't grow them on trees, little brother," AJ replied.

"Yeah, and if they did, you'd probably pick one that was green," Brian joked.

"Or rotten to the core," AJ laughed.

AJ's laughter was cut short when he saw a man riding like the devil himself was after him. Brian saw the man at almost the same time and commented.

"Please don't tell me that guy is bringing trouble with him. That's all we need," Brian said under his breath.

"Maybe we ought to shoot him to keep him from giving us bad news," AJ replied jokingly.

The rider was cutting cross country instead of following the road. When he drew near the Big Spring watering hole he reined up and let his horse drink for some time. When he saw Brian and AJ watching him, he gave them a frantic wave.

"Whew," Brian said, letting out his breath in a rush. "I think he's just in a hurry to get somewhere."

"Yeah, or maybe he has a posse after him," AJ commented only half joking.

"Let's see where he's from and where he's headed," Brian said and they kicked their horses up and rode in the man's direction.

"Howdy," Brian said as they drew near the lone rider.

"Hi, neither one of you gents is a doctor by any chance, are you," the man asked breathlessly?

The two of them looked at one another and then back at the young man, "Nope, why are you in need of one," AJ asked?

"I'm not, but my wife is. She's having a baby and the baby is breach. I don't know what to do, but she's in terrible pain and I gotta find a doctor and quick," the man said with panic in his eyes.

"Maybe that wagon train coming there has someone who could help you," Brian said motioning towards the approaching wagons.

"Maybe they do," the man said and reined his horse around and headed in the wagons direction.

"Hey, I wonder if Julia might know something about a breach birth," AJ said giving a quick look over his shoulder.

"She might. She nursed Brent back to health," Brian said.

"I think a gunshot wound is a little different than a woman having a baby, little brother. Has anyone ever explained the 'birds and the bees' to you," AJ said with a grin.

"Yeah, Pa did but he didn't tell me how that related to men and women; but, I have a pretty good idea of what makes flowers bloom," Brian came back with a chuckle.

They reined around and headed back to meet the wagon. When they rode up to it Brent asked, "What was that guys hurry?"

"His wife is having a baby and its breach. He was looking for a doctor," AJ said.

Raymond D. Mason

"You mean he left his wife to find a doctor out here in the middle of nowhere," Julia said in a shocked voice?

"That's what he said, Julia," AJ replied.

"Oh, my lord; that poor woman could die. Brent, we've got to help her. I've seen breach births before and that baby has got to be turned," Julia said and then added. "I'll take your horse, Brent and go see if I can help that poor woman."

"You won't go alone," Brent said quickly. "Brian, let Julia take your horse and I'll go with her."

"Sure thing," Brian said and stepped down off his horse.

Brent jumped down and ran around to the rear of the wagon and untied his horse while Julia was climbing aboard Brian's. The two of them rode off to talk to the young man who had ridden towards the wagon train.

AJ yelled after the two, "We'll wait for you here."

Brent waved that he'd heard AJ and they soon caught up to the young man. Brian and AJ watched as the three of them talked for a moment and then headed off in the direction of the young couple's homestead.

"I hope Julia can help the woman," Brian said.

"Yeah, me too...Brent can help the young fella pace up and down," AJ said seriously and then grinned.

"Well, I guess we can make ourselves at home while they're gone. How about a pot of coffee," Brian asked?

"Fire it up," AJ replied.

Range War

Jake Hardin and Lee Goodnight packed their saddlebags and bedrolls with supplies and were headed towards Lubbock County within the hour. They both knew that it would be nothing short of a miracle if they were able to find the Sackett brothers. But, they would give it their best effort.

They rode away from the Sackett ranch and headed towards Abilene. They wanted to cover as much distance as they could while it was still light and were more intent on the road ahead than the hilltop off to their right. Marshal Ben Coyle and his deputy were watching the two of them from a distance.

"Ten to one that the two of them are headed towards Lubbock County," Coyle said, getting an agreeing nod from his deputy, Martin Bloom.

"Are we going to follow them," Bloom asked?

"Yep, we'll stay at a distance and see where they head once they get to Abilene. It could be that Sackett has sent them into town for something, but I'm guessing they're taking a message to his boys," Coyle said as he kicked his horse up and moved down the hillside slope with Bloom following him.

"What about supplies, Ben," Bloom said as he galloped up alongside Coyle?

"I've got enough for about four or five days. Do you have anything?"

"I've got my eatin' utensils and a can of peaches is all. Well, my bedroll has some hardtack rolled up in it," Bloom answered.

"We'll be able to pick something up along the way, I'm sure. I don't want to take a chance on losing these guys," Coyle said seriously.

Coyle and Bloom stayed at a safe distance behind Hardin and Goodnight. Riding the ridges they always had the two men in sight. Jake Hardin was a cousin of John Wesley Hardin and, like his cousin, had a sense that told him someone was watching them. He kept looking around which caused Goodnight to question him.

"Are you looking for Comanche or Pawnee sign, Jake," Goodnight asked?

"I don't know what I'm looking for Lee. All I know is I have a feeling we're being watched. Don't you feel it," Hardin asked?

"No, not really; but, I will say that you're making me a little jumpy. I'll keep my eyes peeled for anything out of the ordinary, too," Goodnight stated.

Hardin looked up ahead and saw a dry wash that gave him an idea. He gave Goodnight a quick look and said, "Lee, when we get to that dry wash up ahead, you stay on the road. I'm going to cut off and see if I can locate who it is that's watching us…if anyone is."

Goodnight nodded and when they reached the dry wash did as he had been asked to do. Hardin rode down into the dry wash and reined up near a cottonwood tree. He looked back in the direction they had come, but didn't watch the road as much as he scoured the hillsides.

He didn't have to wait long until he spotted Marshal Coyle and Bloom top a rise about eight hundred yards behind them. Hardin grinned to himself and said, "I thought so."

Range War

Hardin rode out of the dry wash and caught up with Goodnight. It appeared to the marshal and his deputy that Hardin may have stopped to relieve himself and did so in the wash.

"We've got company all right, Lee. I'll bet you a ten spot it's that marshal and his deputy. We'll have to give them the slip once we hit town. That shouldn't be too hard to do though," Jake Hardin grinned.

Raymond D. Mason

18

JULIA SMILED at the woman who was in excruciating pain as she said in a soft, tender voice, "We're going to get that baby turned so you can have it and get rid of this pain at the same time."

The woman was soaking wet and her breathing was fast. Julia went to work doing her best trying to reposition the baby. With the woman screaming in agony, it was hard to concentrate on what needed to be done, but Julia persevered.

The two men; Brent and the woman's husband, Grant; paced up and down outside the room. Brent wore the same worried look on his face as the young man did. They were both wringing their hands and casting quick glances at the door to the bedroom that the two women were behind.

Julia knew that the woman was close to losing consciousness from the severe pain and hoped she could get the baby turned before that happened. There was another problem that Julia thought of also; the umbilical cord. She prayed it wasn't around the baby's neck.

After working for a solid hour, Julia finally got the baby turned around with its feet point down. This wasn't the best position for the birth, but at least it was turned so it could be delivered. Now, however, the umbilical cord problem was very possible.

"Push, honey," Julia said. "You can have your baby now; we've got it turned."

The woman began to push in order to have her baby. With Julia coaxing her every second the woman strained.

"It's coming," Julia said as she pulled slightly on the baby's feet. "Just a little more, honey. It's coming. Push, push; keep pushing."

The delivery took a good ten minutes from the time Julia got the baby turned, but the woman finally gave birth to a little girl. Just as Julia had feared, though, the umbilical cord had wrapped around the baby's neck, but Julia untangled it as soon as she saw the problem.

The woman was exhausted from the ordeal, but Julia's work wasn't finished. The baby wasn't breathing. Julia began moving the baby's arms up and down; over its head and down to its sides.

"Brent, help me," Julia called out loudly.

Brent burst through the door and Julia yelled out, "The baby isn't breathing."

Brent, not knowing anything else to do, grabbed the baby up and began pumping it like it was an accordion. He pumped and pumped with Julia and the young father watching in stunned silence.

Suddenly the baby began to cry. All eyes widened and then smiles exploded across every face in the room. Brent's smile was the widest and most beaming of them all.

"You did it, Brent; you saved that baby's life," Julia said in tearful jubilation.

"I guess I did, huh," Brent said and let out with a laugh. "I did it. I saved this baby's life."

Brent looked down at the wet, crying baby and smiled as he gently touched the baby's cheek. When he looked at the father he had tears in his eyes.

"Here's your baby," Brent said as he handed the baby over to its father. "She's beautiful...and she's alive."

The young man carefully took his daughter and moved over by the bed where his wife was lying. He looked from the baby to the mother and said, "Look, honey, she's okay."

The smile on his face suddenly faded and he said, "Honey...honey; look. The baby is okay."

Julia looked quickly at the mother who had a faint smile on her face with her eyes closed. Julia quickly grabbed the young woman's hand and felt for a pulse. Not finding one she put her head to the woman's chest and listened for a heartbeat. There was none.

Julia looked at Brent and slowly shook her head negatively.

"Honey...honey," the young man said with panic showing in his voice.

Julia's eyes filled with tears and her voice cracked slightly as she said, "She's gone, Grant. It was just too much for her. I'm so sorry."

Julia put her arms around the young man's shoulders and looked at Brent. Brent held a sad look on his face; the joy of saving the baby's life being short lived. He put his hand on Grant's shoulder as well.

Grant stood there stunned and numb. He glanced down at his newborn daughter and swallowed hard as tears began to stream down his face.

"I'll name her Grace; after her mama," Grant said. "Grace Holt...that's pretty don't you think," Grant said and looked at Julia and then at Brent.

"That's a beautiful name," Julia said tearfully and then asked. "What will you do now, Grant?"

"I don't know...I never thought this would...I just don't know," Grant said.

AJ and Brian were leaning back against the wagon wheel when they heard the sound of approaching hoof beats. They both leaned forward so they could see who was coming and when they realized it was Brent they got to their feet.

"What's up," AJ asked, just before they saw Julia seated on the bench seat of the buckboard and holding something in her arms, and the young man driving the team of horses, with Brian's horse tethered to the rear of the buckboard.

"We were able to save the baby, but the baby's mama didn't make it," Brent said just loud enough for them to hear and then looked back at the wagon. "This young fella is going with us. He can't stay out here, that's for sure," he added.

Julia heard Brent's comment and as the buckboard pulled up by where Brian and AJ were now standing added, "That's right; he couldn't possibly stay out here and work his land and take care of a baby at the same time. They were barely making it as it was, so Grant has to make a move.

"We told him he could go with us to California if he wanted to, and I'd take care of the baby. He said he'd have to give it some thought. He has no one out here to help him."

"Grant...you'll have to make up your mind now; would you like to go to California, with us," Brent asked?

Grant looked at Brent through red rimmed eyes and thought for a moment. Finally he made his decision.

"I'd love to go to California with you. I can't bare the thought of staying out here in this lonely place without my Gracie's mother. Yes, if you'll let me, I'll gladly go with you."

"That's settled then; Grant and little Grace are going with us to California," Brent said evenly.

AJ and Brian grinned slightly at the way the decision had come about, but they could tell that's what Julia, Brent, and the new father wanted. First though they would go to the ranch for a proper farewell.

Hardin and Goodnight reached Abilene ahead of the two lawmen. They had hatched a plan for losing the two star packers once they reached town. They stopped at the first saloon they came to and Goodnight climbed off and handed his bridle reins to Hardin.

Hardin rode around to the back of the saloon, leading Goodnight's horse and tied both horses to a support post on a shed. Hardin then went into the saloon, using the back door. By the time he had gotten inside, Marshal Ben Coyle and his deputy had gotten into town, but couldn't see the horses the men were riding.

Instantly Coyle thought the two had ridden on through town, but told his deputy to check the saloons. When Bloom checked the first saloon and found the two men were there he left to tell Coyle. Hardin had been watching the two lawmen from the saloon's doorway and when he saw where they were, motioned for Goodnight to go out the back door.

Hardin followed Goodnight, but stopped at the back door leaving it open just a crack. He waited until he saw the marshal and the deputy enter the saloon and then he and Goodnight mounted up and kicked their horses into a full gallop down the alleyway in back of the businesses.

The two lawmen looked around the barroom and when they didn't see the men, asked the bartender if he knew where they had gone. The bartender motioned towards the back door with a nod, sending the two lawmen running back there to see if they could spot the cowboys. By the time they got outside, the two cowhands were no where to be seen.

"Dad gum it," Coyle said, "Come on, let's get the horses and see if we can pick up their trail. If they're headed for Lubbock County we shouldn't have any trouble finding them."

"We might if they know we're following them," Bloom stated.

"Well, it's obvious they know they're being followed or they wouldn't have pulled this stunt," the marshal snapped.

The two of them went back through the saloon and mounted up. They rode at a leisurely pace out of Abilene and took the main road in the direction of Lubbock County.

This time, however, they were the ones being followed. Hardin and Goodnight had reined up in a grove of cottonwoods and allowed them to pass them by. Now they could follow along and not have to worry about leaving any tracks.

When night fell, the lawmen made camp and kept an eye ahead of them for a glow in the night sky which might indicate another campfire up ahead. It never occurred to either of them to look behind them. Hardin and Goodnight didn't worry one bit about being spotted. If the glow from their fire was seen by the marshal and his deputy they would merely think it was some travelers on their way to who knows where.

Raymond D. Mason

19

LINC SACKETT AND CLAY BUTLER sat at a small rickety table in the only cantina in the settlement with no name. They looked at the other cowhands who were in the bar and after awhile Clay spoke.

"I'm going to walk out and take a look at some of the brands on the horses. I'll be right back," Clay said.

"Yeah, okay Clay. Do you want another beer," Linc asked him?

"Yeah, but this one's on me," Clay said as he walked towards the door.

Clay walked out and checked the brand on each horse at the hitching rail. There were two that had the Circle I-C brand on it. Clay grew tense as he thought that the horses could very well belong to the men responsible for his sister's death.

He walked back inside with a deep frown set between his eyes. He looked around the room and got a few stares back in return. One of the men that took exception to the stare was Johnny Rio.

"What's your problem, man," Rio asked?

"I want to know who is riding the horses wearing the Circle I-C brand tied up out there," Clay said locking his gaze on Rio.

"I'm riding one...why," Rio asked?

"Have you been up to Cottonwood lately," Clay asked?

"No, I ain't been to Cottonwood lately; why do you ask," Rio asked, fishing for more information?

"I'll ask the questions, if you don't mind," Clay snapped.

"Well, I do mind so I guess that settles that, eh."

Linc stood up and moved over next to Clay.

"Aren't you Johnny Rio," Linc asked?

"Yeah, I'm Rio...who are you?"

"The name is Linc Sackett. Weren't you and Jess Latimer pretty tight," Linc asked?

"We were until some Bo-hunk killed him," Rio stated.

"I guess I'm that Bo-hunk you're talking about. I'd say you had better pick the ones you choose to run around with better," Linc said stone faced.

"You'd be Linc Sackett, then," Rio said.

"That's right, Rio."

"I'm sure we'll meet again some time, Sackett. Until then I'll remember what you said about me picking my friends better. Oh, by the way...that goes for you too, if this Bo-hunk is your friend," Rio said looking at Clay.

"You and I are going to lock horns, Rio. I don't know where or when, but I can guarantee you that we'll lock horns sooner or later," Clay said firmly.

Range War

Just then movement at the saloon doors caused the patrons to look that way. A tall man walked in that anyone could tell had been in the saddle for some time. He stopped and looked around the room.

Clay got a grin on his face as he recognized the man. Clay let out a laugh that caused the big man to look his way.

"Well, I'll be...hello Clay," the man said with a huge smile of his own.

"Quirt Adams, you old horse thief...how are you doing? And, I might add, what are you doing down here? Who's running the ranch," Clay asked.

Rio looked hard at Adams. He'd heard of the big rancher who had been responsible for putting a number of his friends in their grave.

"So this is the big, bad Quirt Adams I've heard so much about," Rio snapped.

Quirt's grin dropped quickly at the tone of Rio's voice. He looked the smallish man up and down and then asked, "Who rattled your cage, hoss?"

"I guess you did, big man. And I don't like anybody rattling my cage; if you get my drift," Rio said sullenly.

"Don't push it, pardner; I didn't come in here looking for trouble; only a beer. But, if it's trouble you're dealing in then let's get it on," Quirt said slowly and pushed his slicker back so he could reach his pistol without interference.

Rio looked at him for a minute and then at Linc and Clay. He slowly shook his head and stated, "Not now; the odds are a little against me. I'll choose the time and place."

"Just make sure it's not behind me and when I'm not looking," Quirt said with a steely eyed stare.

Rio grinned and said, "Don't worry...you'll see it coming; I want you to see it coming."

With that Rio downed the rest of his whiskey and walked slowly to the door, glaring at the three men he'd had words with as he moved by them. Another man got up and followed Rio out, but offered no comment.

"Who put a burr under that guy's saddle," Quirt asked?

"That was Johnny Rio, Quirt," Clay said and then looked towards Linc. "Say, Quirt, I'd like to introduce you to Linc Sackett. Linc, meet Quirt Adams, one of the biggest ranchers in the Springville area."

Quirt gave Linc a questioning look and asked, "You're not related to Jubal Sackett are you?"

"He's my uncle. Why do you know Uncle Jubal," Linc asked?

"Yeah, he and I have done some business from time to time. A good man, I must say. It's nice to make your acquaintance, Linc," Quirt said and extended his hand.

"Same here, Quirt," Linc smiled. "How'd you pick up the name Quirt, if you don't mind my asking?"

"No, I don't mind. It was given to me by the man who found me along the trail and raised me as his own. He said anyone who was tough as leather and tightly wound should be named Quirt and that's what I've gone by ever since," Quirt laughed.

"Let me buy you cowboys a drink," Quirt said. "Hey barkeep, set 'em up for me and my friends."

Range War

"Why does your name sound so familiar to me," Linc asked as the bartender set a beer in front of each of them?

"Maybe it had something to do with Raul Ortega and his gang. We had quite a showdown up in Springville a few years back. I danged near lost my wife because of it, too," Quirt offered.

"That's it; I knew that name sounded familiar. Weren't you also involved with some 'Night Riders' up your way," Linc asked?

"I was, yes. We're still having some repercussions over that little incident. It'll all work its self out, though. It always does. It's like my wife says, 'a hundred years from now I won't remember a thing about it.' As you can tell, I'm married to a really smart woman," Quirt laughed.

Clay laughed, as did Linc, then Clay asked, "What brings you down here, Quirt; you didn't say?"

"I just delivered one hundred horses to some cavalrymen who are going to take them to Camp Thomas and have an order for fifty more. I'll be back down this way in another month or so to bring them down. That's why I'm buying, so drink hearty men," Quirt said with a laugh.

"So how do you and Clay know one another," Linc asked?

"That's a good question," Quirt started. "Clay used to work for me and when he had saved enough to put some money down on his own ranch, I gave him fifty head of cattle to get a start. So with fifty head of prime beef, he became a horse rancher," Quirt said and then laughed along with Clay and Linc.

"So, Clay...you know why I'm down here, what are you doing down here? This is a long way from Cottonwood," Quirt asked?

Clay grew serious as he thought of how he wanted to tell Quirt about his sister.

"Remember my sister, Emma? She took a job in the bank at Cottonwood a few years back. Well, not long ago there was a holdup and the three men that robbed the bank shot and killed her as they made their escape.

"I learned from a witness that he'd seen the brand on the horses the men were riding and remembered seeing them down here. I came down to find the men and either take them back for trial or kill them where they stand; whichever way they want it," Clay said.

"Oh, Clay, I'm so sorry to hear that. I remember reading about the bank holdup, but the article I read just said that one of the tellers was shot and killed. The article didn't even say if it was a man or a woman," Quirt said with a pained look on his face.

"Tonight I noticed two horses tied up outside had that same brand; the Circle I-C, but I don't think the ones riding them were involved. Not according to the description given by the bank president and four other witnesses," Clay said and then added. "In fact one of the men riding one of the horses carrying that brand was Rio; and when I asked him if he'd been to Cottonwood lately, said he hadn't."

"You don't really think the men responsible are going to admit it, do you Clay," Quirt asked?

Range War

"No, but I need more proof. Someone knows who the men are and it's just a matter of time until they speak up. When I know for sure who they are, I'll go after them," Clay said firmly.

Quirt knew Clay and knew that he was a careful man. If it was him, he'd shoot anyone riding a horse with that brand and take his chances that he got the guilty parties. Well, at least that was the way he used to be before he got married to Abigail. Quirt had changed a lot due to his love for her.

"Where are you staying, Quirt," Linc asked, changing the subject?

"I'm camped just out of town here. I sent the men who came down with me back to the ranch and gave them each twenty dollars for the good job they did and they headed for Tucson. I hope they're back at the ranch when I get there, but who knows," Quirt laughed.

"We have an empty bunk in the bunkhouse, Quirt, if you'd like to bed down there tonight. It will sure beat sleeping on the ground...not by much, but some," Linc offered. "I don't think our foreman would mind. And, I know the ranch owner won't mind, he lives back east," Linc then added.

"If the foreman won't mind, then I'd love to bunk with you fellas tonight. I'll be getting an early start home in the morning and since this was the nearest cantina around figured to stop here and then move on in the morning. How far is it to your ranch," Quirt asked?

"It's only about five, six miles from here. We'll have another beer and then head back there," Clay said giving Linc a quick wink. "You did say you were buying, didn't you Quirt?"

Quirt laughed, "I see you haven't changed since we last seen each other. Yeah, I'm well heeled," Quirt said.

Two men seated in the cantina overheard Quirt say he was well heeled and gave each other a quick glance. They'd also heard him say he wanted to get an early start for home the next morning. The two put their heads together and spoke very softly.

"Do you know what ranch these two hombres work for," one of the men asked?

"Yes, I do. I tried to get a job there once, but they weren't hiring. We can be there in the morning when the big one leaves. If he's got as much money as he says he does, we could be rich men this time tomorrow night," the other man said casting a quick glance at Quirt.

20

QUIRT ADAMS bunked in the bunkhouse with Linc and Clay and was up before the crack of dawn with the working cowhands. Buck Benton hadn't objected to Quirt spending the night in the bunkhouse and was glad he stayed for breakfast.

Buck had heard of Quirt and some of his exploits and was honored to meet the man. When they got finished with breakfast Buck wrapped up six biscuits for Quirt to take with him on his ride back to his ranch. Quirt thanked him and told the others goodbye.

Outside, Quirt told Clay he hoped he found the men who had killed Emma and if there was ever anything he could do to help him, be sure and get in touch with him. He told Linc what a pleasure it was to meet a family member of Jubal Sackett and then hit the trail.

The two men from the cantina had camped on a slight rise so they could see the ranch house where Quirt had spent the night. As he rode away they mounted up and, keeping out of sight, rode to the spot they had chosen to ambush the big rancher.

Quirt felt good after a good nights sleep and his horse was well rested and ready to travel. Quirt kept it at a nice easy gait and was enjoying the cool of the morning; knowing full well that the sun would soon burn off the cool of the night air.

He had traveled about three miles from the ranch house when the two men jumped him. If it hadn't been for a covey of quail the ambush might have been successful. The quail, however, alerted Quirt to the fact that someone was in the dry wash.

Quirt first thought of Apache Indians when the quail took flight. He quickly reined his horse away from the wash and up a slight hill. He watched the dry wash with a keen eye and when he saw the glisten of sun off the barrel of the Henry rifle, he leaned forward and kicked his horse into a full run.

The bullet whistled over Quirt's back and the second shot kicked up dust off a sand stone in front of Quirt. He had never seen the ones doing the shooting, but fired his Colt .44 in the direction of the dry wash.

As he got out of range, the two bushwhackers took to their animals and gave chase. Quirt let his horse have its head and the big roan seemed to separate from the bushwhackers with each step. Quirt looked over his shoulder and saw the two men giving chase.

Quirt actually felt relief when he saw that his 'would be bushwhackers' were bandits and not Apache Indians. He saw a large rock formation in the distance and headed the roan towards it.

Quirt had been in worse situations than this and was aware of what he had to do. The first thing he wanted to do was make sure the men couldn't come at him from anywhere but in front.

When he reached the rock formation he grabbed his Winchester '73 from his saddle holster and got between two large rocks. He laid the Winchester atop a rock in front of him and waited for the two men to get in range.

The men, having seen Quirt take to the rocks, split off; one going to the left and one going to the right. Now if they could just get him in crossfire they would soon be the richer for it. Of course, Quirt wasn't about to let them do it that easy.

There was very little cover for the men to use as shields and to get to the nearest rocks would require crossing a clear area. Quirt measured the distance of each clear spot and aimed at the one that would require the least amount of time to cross. He waited patiently for the man to try and make it across the clearing.

Glancing towards the larger clearing to make sure he didn't give the second man too much of an advantage, Quirt was slightly caught off guard when the first man started for the rocks.

Quirt had to make a snap shot, but he made it count. He hit the man and dropped him to the ground. The man didn't move, which turned Quirt's attention to the second man and the larger clearing.

The fact that the first man had been hit must have caused his partner to have second thoughts about going one on one against Quirt. As Quirt held his rifle ready, he saw the second man hightailing it back in the direction from which they'd come.

Quirt stepped out from between the rocks and looked for his horse. He spotted it about fifty yards away feeding on some Jensen weed. He gave a whistle and the horse came trotting over to him. Quirt rode over to where the man he'd shot lay.

The man was still alive, but in bad shape. Quirt looked at the man and recognized him from the cantina the night before.

"Why'd you try it, man," Quirt asked?

"The money...what else," the man struggled to say.

"Was it worth it?"

"No, not hardly," the man said just before his head dropped to one side and he died.

"Foolish, foolish hombre," Quirt said.

When Quirt saw the man's horse tied to some scrub brush he walked over to it. As he started to take the saddle and bridle off the horse he noticed the horse's brand. It was the Circle I-C brand.

Quirt pursed his lips thoughtfully and then nodded his head before spooking the horse, leaving the saddle, bridle, and blanket on the ground. He figured the horse would go back to the ranch and the other bushwhacker would know what had happened to his cohort.

Quirt mounted his horse and headed out on his way back to his ranch just out of Springville. He felt sure that he would be seeing both Clay Butler and Linc Sackett again. He hoped so anyway.

Marshal Ben Coyle and his deputy rode in the direction of Lubbock County but were perplexed by

Range War

the fact they could find no sign of two horses heading that way. They could find plenty of horse tracks, but none that seemed to be heading towards Lubbock County.

Meanwhile, behind the two lawmen Hardin and Goodnight were enjoying a leisurely ride that allowed them plenty of time to talk to people who might have come from Lubbock County. They talked to no one who had, however.

The two cowboys had just reached Camp Springs when they came upon a lone wagon that had been burned. They couldn't find any sign of the people belonging to the wagon and figured that they'd either managed to get away from the marauding Indians that had attacked them, or had been taken captive.

Hardin looked at the wagon and said, "If this was Indians who did this, they were armed with rifles. There's not a single arrow in this wagon."

"It was Indians all right, Jake. Look at these pony tracks; unshod," Goodnight said pointing towards the ground.

"What do you think, Comanche or Pawnee?"

"I'd say this far north it could be Pawnee...maybe Kiowa. It looks like a small war party," Goodnight answered.

"We'll have to keep our eyes peeled. I'd hate to ride into an ambush," Hardin said.

"Let's get out of here. Whoever was in this wagon are long gone by now," Goodnight said.

The two kicked up their horses and hit an easy gallop away from the wagon. They had traveled about five miles when Goodnight held up his hand.

"What is it," Hardin asked?

"We've been traveling the same way as those Indian pony tracks and they just peeled off and headed over that rise. I think I'll ride up there and see if I can see them," Goodnight said as he reined his horse up the slope.

Hardin waited and watched as Goodnight made the ride to the crest of hill. When he saw how abruptly Goodnight came to a halt and backed his horse up, he knew his friend had seen something very interesting.

Goodnight climbed off his horse and held the reins as he crawled back up to the top of the ridge. No more than two hundred yards away were the people who had been traveling in the wagon that had been burned. They were in the midst of eight Kiowa warriors.

Goodnight motioned for Hardin to join him, but to stay low. Hardin rode half way up the hill before climbing off his horse and going the rest of the way on foot. When he reached Goodnight he peered over the crest and saw the captives and the Kiowa.

Hardin whispered, "Is that all the Kiowa there are? There're no more standing guard are there, Lee?"

"I haven't seen any. I see two women and one man, but that's all as far as the captives go. How do you want to work this?"

Hardin looked the situation over and then smiled as he said, "Work your way around to those trees on the right. I'll work my way to the rocks on the left so we have them in crossfire. Give me time to get to where the Kiowa have their horses tied though.

Range War

"I'll cut their horses loose and when I get back to the rocks we'll both open up on the ones nearest us. If any of the Indians go for the captives we'll turn our guns on them. I think if we take them by surprise they'll forget about the captives. Take good aim and don't miss," Hardin said.

"I'll cover you while you work your way to where their horses are. If any of them spot you I'll open up on them," Goodnight stated.

"I hope so, Lee," Hardin grinned.

Hardin stayed low as he made his way around to where the Indian's horses were tethered to a rope line. Once he'd managed to loosen the rope reins of the horses he moved towards the rocky area.

He made it without being seen and once behind the rocks he aimed at the Indian nearest him. He slowly squeezed the trigger and the shooting began. Fortunately the captives knew what to do when Hardin and Goodnight opened up on the Kiowa. They took off in a dead run towards the nearest cover. When the shooting started the Indian ponies all bolted.

Hardin got two of the Kiowa on his side and Goodnight got three on his side. The other three Indians made a mad dash for their horses only to find them gone. They turned and opened fire in the direction of the gunfire behind them.

When Hardin and Goodnight saw the Indians throw their rifles down and start running they let them go. Obviously the Indians had run out of ammunition and were clearing out.

Raymond D. Mason

21

THE THREE CAPTIVES came out of their hiding place once the shooting had stopped and they saw the two men who had saved them. The man had a huge grin on his face and the two women had fear etched into their eyes.

"It's okay, folks," Hardin said. "Everything is okay; you're safe now."

"We don't know how to thank you men. We were jumped by surprise and taken prisoner. I don't know why; they came out of no where," the man said in a rush.

The women remained silent and continued to look around them anxiously. Goodnight watched the women and thought something seemed out of the ordinary but didn't know what it was.

"You didn't see another one of our party did you," the man asked?

"Oh, there was another person with you," Hardin asked?

"Yes, my business partner. He jumped off the wagon when they attacked us and ran into the underbrush. One of the bucks went after him, but he didn't bring him back. I'm afraid he killed him," the man said.

"We didn't see anyone else. I'll go and see if I can locate him when we leave here," Hardin said.

"What were you folks hauling," Goodnight asked?

The man looked quickly at the women and then grinned, "Uh, Bibles. We were hauling Bibles. Not too many, mind you, just a couple of cases."

"Bibles, eh; where were you taking them," Goodnight asked curiously?

"To our...uh, small gathering of believers," the man said nervously.

Goodnight nodded his head slowly and then asked, "Now, what were you really hauling in that wagon. It wasn't Bibles, so what was it?"

Hardin was watching Goodnight and wondering why his voice had taken on the tone it had. He looked at the man and could see the nervousness on his face.

The man finally gave a look of disgust and said tightly, "Whiskey...we sold the Indians some whiskey."

Goodnight looked quickly at the women and asked, "Is that right, ladies?"

The women, neither of which looked like the typical wife of a cowboy or a farmer, looked at the man and the older one said, "They were selling whiskey to the Indians...and guns."

Range War

"That's what I thought," Goodnight said. "So what happened...they got drunk and didn't want to pay you; is that it?"

The man glared at the women and snapped angrily, "Yeah, something like that. They wanted to take the women with them back to their camp. When they got rough is when my partner, the coward, ran off into the brush and left me to deal with them alone."

"I'll see if I can round up a couple of horses for you. Consider yourselves lucky that your scalps aren't hanging on some wikkiup pole about now. If I was you I'd get to a town as quickly as possible. The ones who got away may come back with some more braves. And, they'll be looking for you," Goodnight said with a frown.

He rode off to see if he could find a couple of the Indian's horses he'd spooked. He was back shortly with two horses and told them that two of them would have to double up.

"Come on Jake, we've got a lot of ground to make up," Goodnight said and then looked at the man with a hard look. "I should turn you over to the nearest marshal and let the law deal with you, but we have some pressing business to take care of now.

"I have nothing but contempt for your kind of low life. You'd cut your own mother's throat for the gold in her teeth. If I ever run across you again...well, let's just hope I don't. Now you take your two saloon girls and skedaddle out of here."

Hardin didn't say much, he just looked at his partner with a half grin on his face. He'd never known Goodnight to be anything but an easy going sort; he was seeing another side of Lee today, however.

They watched as the three mounted up on the Indian ponies and rode off in the direction of Abilene. Hardin grinned and looked at Goodnight.

"How'd you figure them to be whiskey and gun runners to the Indians? I didn't see anything that would make me think that."

"It was the whole story that made me curious. If it was an ambush like the man said, why hadn't they killed them? Why take them captive; especially the man. His partner leaving them to the mercy of the Indians, I didn't buy either. There may not have even been another man along. I think the women were to seal the deal.

"Another thing was when he said they were hauling Bibles. Did he look like a man well versed in the Bible to you? I doubt it. And I looked at his clothes. He was a businessman; his clothes were only dusty because of what the Kiowa had put him through. Take that dust away and that guy was well dressed. It was just a lot of little things made me suspicious," Goodnight explained.

"I don't have any use for a gun runner...or a whiskey runner for that matter. They cause more of a threat to the white man than some Indian tribes do," Hardin agreed.

Range War

Black Jack Haggerty reined up in front of a cantina on the banks of the Pecos River; a good watering hole for cattle herds on their way to market. Hot and dusty, Haggerty tied up at the small hitching rail and dragged himself inside the bar.

The tired bad man flopped down in a chair and waited for a young Mexican woman to come over and take his order. She wore a peasant's blouse with one sleeve pulled down over her shoulder and was obviously advertising her main profession by showing a lot of bosom.

Haggerty eyed her up and down, focusing mainly on her exposure. He slowly looked up into the dark brown eyes of the young woman. He grinned slightly and said, "Beer...Cerveza."

She gave him a sleepy eyed invitation and then swung around and walked to the bar. The bartender said something to her in Spanish and she laughed as she looked back in Haggerty's direction.

The young woman returned with a beer that was mildly cool and sat it on the table in front of him. Haggerty once again eyed her half exposed breast and then tossed a double eagle on the table top.

The woman eyed the money and then smiled at Haggerty as she slowly reached across him to pick the coin up. She let her half exposed breast brush the side of Haggerty's face as she took the coin.

"You can keep the change, honey; you know what I want," he said looking up into her face.

The woman looked down at him and gave a head nod towards a curtain behind the bar. She slowly walked away with Haggerty watching her every move. When she reached the bar, she said something else to the bartender in Spanish and then walked behind the curtain. Before letting the curtain fall shut, however, the woman pulled the other shoulder of her blouse down showing her bare back.

Haggerty got up and took his bottle of beer and headed for the curtain. The bartender gave Haggerty a knowing grin and a head nod as he reached the end of the bar. Haggerty pulled the curtain back and the woman was just climbing into a small bed; she was completely naked.

Haggerty looked around the room and set the bottle on a table near the door. He began to get undressed and when he had removed his gun belt and holster and draped it over the back of a chair, the bartender suddenly jumped him from behind.

The bartender was able to throw Haggerty to the floor, but in the process knocked the chair over that held his gun belt. Haggerty hit the floor hard, but spotted his gun and grabbed it from its holster.

The bartender grabbed a small club that was leaning against the wall and raised it up over his head. Before he could slam it down on Haggerty's head, Jack shot the man right between the eyes.

The woman was screaming at the top of her lungs and Haggerty swung the gun around and fired one shot at her; hitting her in the chest between her openly exposed breasts. The bullet killed her instantly.

"You no good dirty...," Haggerty cursed as he scrambled to his feet and slung his gun belt over his shoulder.

Range War

There would be no rest for the man on the dodge here. He rushed out of the cantina just as several cowboys rode up. They'd heard the shots but didn't know what had happened. Haggerty didn't wait to explain. He swung into the saddle and rode away in a cloud of dust.

22

BRENT SACKETT looked sadly at his brothers and shook his head, "I can't go back to Abilene to see Ma and Pa. I'd like to, but I just can't. I've got to get out of Texas as soon as I can. Please tell them I'm sorry, and that I'll get in touch with them once we get settled in California."

Brian nodded slowly as did AJ. They knew that it would be too dangerous for him to try and visit the ranch with the law coming around and seeing if he had made contact with any of them.

"All we can say, Brent, is that we understand and wish you the very best. We'll explain everything to the folks," Brian said thoughtfully.

"Brent, you have a real fine woman there. Take good care of her and may God go with you," AJ added.

"I know I do, AJ; she's a life saver. As soon as we get settled somewhere out west I want us to find a good church and really become a family. And, it's going to happen because she just told me that she's expecting. So, I guess the next time we see one another you'll both be uncles," Brent smiled.

"Unless it's a girl, then we'll both be aunts," Brian said with a serious look.

AJ and Brent looked at him with dumbfounded looks for a moment and then all three broke into laughter. It was so good to laugh together like they had before the War had come along and separated them.

"Are you turning back this morning," AJ asked after they'd enjoyed their good laugh?

"Yeah, no need in going on. We'll join up with a wagon train headed west. Julia is in hog heaven taking care of that baby. I think Grant will be good as a cover for me. The law won't be looking for Brent Sackett with a wife, a baby, and a young man traveling by wagon, I'm sure," Brent stated.

"Well, we're saddled and ready to go, Brent. Take care, brother. We all love you and we'll be praying for you," Brian said.

"Yeah, and keep us posted about our relationship to the little one," AJ said getting a chuckle from the other two.

The two of them climbed into their saddles and rode over to where Julia was with the baby. Grant was standing by her and looked up when the two rode up. They smiled down at Julia and Brian said, "We're heading out, Julia. We just want to thank you for what all you've done for Brent and the Sackett family. You gave Brent back to us. We'll always love you for that."

"That goes double for me, honey. Take extra special care of yourself. Brent just told us about your blessed event," AJ added.

"I knew he would. Thank you both for being so understanding. I was afraid you'd look down on me for falling for Brent so soon after my husband was killed," Julia said softly.

"Love doesn't use a schedule. It can happen in a heart beat," AJ replied, getting an agreeing nod from Brian.

"Grant... take care my friend," Brian said to Grant Holt.

"Let us know how you're doing from time to time would you," AJ offered?

"I will. Thanks for everything," Grant said evenly.

The two brothers swung around and kicked their horses into a slow gallop. They both gave a final wave to Brent, Julia, Grant, and baby Grace. Their next stop would be the Sackett ranch. If anyone came looking for Brent they'd send them to a grave in Sundown, Texas.

They were about halfway to Abilene when they ran across the marshal and his deputy. When the marshal saw that they were by themselves he pretended to be out that way for some other reason than hoping to find Brent.

"Well, howdy, Marshal...what brings you out this way," AJ asked with a grin?

"Did you boys meet up with Brent somewhere," the marshal asked?

"Brent...no, we came out here to see a man about buying some of his cattle. He decided to tough this dry spell out, so we're going home," Brian stated.

Range War

"I'll get him; it's just a matter of time," Marshal Coyle said.

"Marshal, we just ran into a man from Sundown and he said that Brent had been killed and is buried up there. If we had managed to find him, we'd only find a grave somewhere. I think you'd better give it up; we certainly have," Brian said seriously.

Just then AJ looked off into the distance and saw two men on horseback. It was Hardin and Goodnight. He motioned to Brian, which caused the marshal and his deputy to look in their direction.

"Well, I'll be..." the marshal said under his breath.

"Hey, Ben; that looks like the two guys we were supposed to be following. How did they get behind us," the deputy asked?

When Hardin and Goodnight rode up to the four of them, they gave a nod and Goodnight said, "Are we glad to see you, Marshal. We ran across some gun and whiskey runners to the Indians a ways back and left three of them riding two Indian ponies and head back to Abilene. Maybe you should check them out."

"We've got more pressing business than that," Coyle snapped. "We're heading for Sundown." He then looked at Brian and said, "Thanks for the tip on where Brent is. I know that old trick; tell someone to look where you don't want them to look. Well, that won't work. Come on, let's head north," he said to his deputy.

169

Brian, AJ, Hardin, and Goodnight watched the two lawmen head north for Sundown and Brian and AJ smiled widely.

"Let's head for home, guys," AJ said and kicked up his horse. The others did likewise. Next stop the Sackett ranch.

Quirt Adams made it to his ranch without any further incidents and found the men who'd helped him move the herd of horses south were back and at work. He was glad he'd run into Clay Butler while on the trip. He didn't know it, but he would be seeing his old friend a lot sooner than he could imagine.

Haggerty continued on his way to Arizona, this time without the company of his old friend, Frank 'Four Fingers' Jordan. Hard times were about to catch up with the Texas bad man, but he didn't know it.

Clay Butler would soon find out who the men were who had killed his sister during the bank holdup in Cottonwood. It would lead him close to losing his own life, but he would willingly die if it meant avenging his sister, Emma.

Linc Sackett would soon run afoul of some friends of the men that he'd killed when he caught them stealing cattle. There would be enough of them that it would require some help from some of his own friends.

Brent and Julia would soon join up with a wagon train on its way to California and meet some people who would become close friends. They would also meet up with someone who knew Brent from his days on the run in Texas.

Brian and AJ would become involved in a manhunt for men who had attempted to kill their father and almost succeeded. It would take them deep into Mexico where they would encounter Mexican bandits and barely escape with their lives.

The End

Look for the next book in the Sackett Series
"Five Faces West"

Raymond D. Mason

Books by This Author

Mysteries

8 Seconds to Glory
A Motive for Murder
A Tale of Tri-Cities
A Walk on the Wilder Side
Beyond Missing
Blossoms in the Dust
Brotherhood of the Cobra
Counterfeit Elvis: (1)
Corrigan
If Looks Could Kill
Illegal Crossing
In the Chill of the Night
Most Deadly Intentions
Murder on the Oregon Express
Odor in the Court
On a Lonely Mountain Road
Return of 'Booger' Doyle
Send in the Clones
Shadows of Doubt
Sleazy Come, Sleazy Go
Suddenly, Murder
The Mystery of Myrtle Creek
The Secret of Spirit Mountain
The Tootsie Pop Kid
The Woman in the Field
Too Late To Live

Westerns

Aces and Eights
Across the Rio Grande
Beyond the Great Divide
Beyond the Picket Wire
Brimstone; End of the Trail
Day of the Rawhiders
Five Faces West
Four Corners Woman
Incident at Medicine Bow
King of the Barbary Coast
Laramie
Last of the Long Riders
Man from Silver City
Night of the Blood Red Moon
Night Riders
Purple Dawn
Rage at Del Rio
Range War
Rebel Pride
Return to Cutter's Creek
Ride the Hard Land
Ride the Hellfire Trail
Showdown at Lone Pine
Streets of Durango: *Lynching*
Streets of Durango: *Shootings*
Tales of Old Arizona
The Long Ride Back
Three Days to Sundown
Yellow Sky, Black Hawk